WISHING ON A STAR

A Christmas Anthology

Published by Accent Press Ltd 2014

ISBN 9781786156006

CONTENTS

Comfort and Joy

Christina Jones

Of course, they all agreed, nodding sagely, and stirring their terminally weak tea, it was very sad, and life in The Terrace would never be the same, but it was for the best really, wasn't it? Ivy would be cared for properly now. She'd have someone watching over her. Nurses and carers day and night.

Naturally, it was shocking that she'd been struck down so early. Well, Ivy wasn't much past eighty, was she? And eighty was the new sixty, so all the papers kept saying. Practically middle-aged. But even if she couldn't get about much any more, at least Ivy still had all her marbles, so to speak. She'd still be able to read her books and watch her soaps and do her crossword puzzles and word-searches, and the nursing home was top of the tree, so it certainly wasn't the worst way to face the autumn years of such an eventful and active life.

It was a shame, they all said, tinkling teaspoons into their saucers, that Ivy's family couldn't have taken her in. But then, what with her walking frame and needing to sleep downstairs, maybe the nursing home was the best answer.

They'd all go and visit her, naturally. Well, maybe not until Christmas was over, because there were so many other things to do, and to be honest, Ivy would probably be kept busy with in-house carol concerts and little pantomimes put on by the staff, and that sort of thing. They'd pop cards and a little gift into the post for her. That was probably best.

Hilda and Myrtle drained their teacups, politely refused Elsie's offer of a refill, and creaked slowly to their feet.

''Course,' Elsie lifted down their serviceable winter coats and sorted scarves and gloves and snug woolly hats, 'there's the problem of the house.'

'House?' Myrtle paused in winding her scarf tightly round her throat as if she had miles to go instead of just next-door-but-one. 'Ivy's house?'

'Ivy's house,' Elsie nodded. 'What'll happen to it? She never bought it, did she?'

No, Myrtle and Hilda shook their heads. She never did. They had, of course. But they'd still had their husbands then. Husbands who understood that little leaflet, *The Right to Buy*. Ivy's Bill had passed on way back in the seventies. Sadly, she'd been a widow for longer than she'd been a wife. Not that Ivy had ever let it get her down. She was a cheerful soul, was Ivy.

They looked at each other.

Ivy's house …

'I suppose it's still council, then?' Hilda ventured.

'You don't call it that any more.' Elsie was up on these things. Dennis, her eldest, worked in planning. 'Housing Association took over years back – it's called social housing now, not council.'

'Ah,' Myrtle struggled into her astrakhan coat and sucked her teeth. 'So that means they could put, well, anybody in there?'

'Anybody,' Elsie confirmed with a gloomy nod. 'Absolutely anybody.'

It was unthinkable. They'd all moved into The Terrace at the same time, young wives with their lives ahead of them. They'd been friends and shared

3

everything for decades. And now the Housing Association could put just *anybody* into Ivy's house.

'There must be someone we can speak to,' Hilda puffed as she zipped up her bootees. 'Explain to them that The Terrace is special. Say that we need someone who will keep up standards and what have you.'

The others nodded vigorously. They'd never let their standards drop. The competition had always been fierce. Doorsteps gleamed, windows dazzled, door-knockers sparkled, flowerbeds blazed. They couldn't have just *anybody* living in Ivy's house.

'I'll speak to our Dennis and see if he can pull any strings. Put in a good word, you know,' Elsie said. 'He'll probably nip round with a card and a little what-not before Christmas.'

'You're not going to him for The Day, then?' Hilda and Myrtle had reached the front door.

'No.' Elsie flushed and briskly straightened her shoulders. 'Caroline thought they'd have a quiet time this year – just them and the children – they might be able to fit me in on Boxing Day, mind. What about you?'

'Peter and Susan are going to a hotel,' Myrtle fiddled with her gloves.

'And mine seem to have so many things planned – office dos, parties with their friends, they're very busy …' Hilda studied Elsie's hall carpet. It was multi-coloured swirls and very loud. 'I said not to worry, I'd be fine on my own …'

'Ah well,' Elsie pulled open the front door, letting in a blast of icy air that could have come straight from

4

Siberia, 'that's youngsters, for you. Still, only a week to go and Christmas will be all over. It's not the same as it was. And at least we're luckier than Ivy.'

'Ah, we've got our health and strength,' Myrtle nodded, 'and that's the best present any of us could ask for.' She shivered, squinting at Elsie. 'Now, don't you go forgetting to mention Ivy's house to your Dennis. He'll know what to do.'

They said their goodbyes then, scuttling along the windswept terrace in the freezing late afternoon, not looking at Ivy's house, with its dark, sightless windows, its cold, smokeless chimney, its air of happy memories drenched in tears.

'Mine?' Holly Winters stared hard at the door key in her hand, then stared again across the desk. 'Mine?'

'Yours,' Mr Barker nodded. This was one of the very few pleasant things about his job. 'You ticked all our boxes, your bid was the best, and the workmen have just finished. It's a nice little home, Miss Winters. It's only got two bedrooms which was why it was unsuitable for most of the families on our list. There's a cooker and a fridge and all the basic necessities, but no central heating, I'm afraid. Still, it's just in time for you and – er –' he looked at his screen, 'little – um – Star to be there for Christmas.'

Holly shifted the toddler on her lap, ran her fingers over the key in disbelief, and let the tears roll unashamedly down her cheeks.

Mr Barker looked rather embarrassed and groped in the desk drawer for the box of tissues specially kept for tearful clients. They weren't usually happy tears.

He liked this girl. She really deserved the house. She'd been in bed-and-breakfast ever since the child had been born. He'd met her several times before and liked her sense of dignity and her polite manner even when he'd had to tell her that her online housing application had been unsuccessful. Politeness and dignity were two things that were frequently missing in his job. Holly Winters had them in spades.

Painfully thin herself and never dressed warmly, she made sure that – er – little Star was always clean and plump and well muffled in this bitter weather. And Miss Winters had always been patient and had never made any demands. She'd always accepted that her wait for a home would be a long one. Yes, Holly Winters deserved a break. And it was very comforting to know she'd be under her own roof for Christmas.

'Is it all right if I move in straight away?' Holly asked. 'I'm not sure what the procedure is …'

'Straight away,' Mr Barker confirmed. 'We can get you help with second-hand furniture and things, if you like.'

'Thank you,' Holly said proudly, 'but I've got my basic odds and ends in storage, so Star and I have everything we need. We wouldn't want to take anything we weren't entitled to.'

'No, of course not.' Mr Barker rose to his feet and shook Holly's free hand. He hoped he hadn't insulted her. 'And good luck, Miss Winters. I hope you'll be very happy in The Terrace.'

'I'm sure I shall.' Holly smiled through the tears.

'Thank you so much for your help.'

She didn't notice the iciness of the wind, or the threatening ochre sky, or the needle-sting of sleet in the air as she left the housing office. Holly Winters could only feel warmth and happiness; see only peace and security. At last.

Only three days until Christmas. Star would wake up in her own bedroom for the first time. Holly would be able to pack a sock with little bits and pieces and watch her daughter's eyes sparkle with festive magic as her tiny fingers unwrapped each one. Star wouldn't put a price on her presents. They would be given and received with love. The purest emotion of all.

'Star, sweetie,' Holly looked down at her child as she toddled trustingly beside her. 'This is going to be the best Christmas ever. Let's go home, shall we? Home ...'

Star giggled with delight as Holly waltzed her along the High Street, and even the most jaded shopper stopped, stared and smiled at the skinny fair-haired girl in her worn jeans and flimsy jacket with the laughing, ruddy-faced child clinging to her hand. Never mind 'oh, what on earth can we get for your mother *this* year?'. This mother and child brought back memories of rustling paper, Christmas bells pealing across the silent frozen countryside, carols and prayers ...

'She's an unmarried mother!' Myrtle hissed. 'And blatant about it!'

'I think you have to say single parent these days, actually,' Elsie sipped her sweet sherry and grimaced.

It wasn't a named brand. Hilda had always been tight that way. 'It's more politically correct.'

Myrtle sighed heavily and pulled a face.

'Anyway,' Elsie continued, 'my Dennis said it was all cut and dried. They'd allocated the house ages ago. As soon as Ivy had had her assessment. It was all done online – ridiculous if you ask me – and there weren't many people interested because of it only being two bedrooms. There was nothing anyone could do.'

Myrtle bridled. 'Only two bedrooms! Why, we brought up our entire families in only two bedrooms, didn't we?'

They all nodded. They had.

'And now they want umpteen bedrooms and more than one bathroom,' Hilda added. 'I've seen it on the telly shows. They turn down properly decent houses because they've only got one bathroom … Madness!'

An air of gloom descended on Hilda's rather prim parlour. There were no decorations. Half a dozen Christmas cards leaned heavily on the mantelpiece. It was Christmas Eve.

'Disgusting, I call it,' Hilda played with a rather overdone mince pie. It would never have passed muster with Mary Berry, that's for sure. 'After all, what does a *young person* know about The Terrace? And she's probably no better than she ought to be. There'll be men in there morning, noon, and night, you mark my words.'

Myrtle choked on her mince pie crumbs, and took a swig of sherry. It didn't help much.

They sat in mournful silence, each thinking of other

Christmases when none of them would have believed they'd ever be old and alone. And they thought about Holly Winters in Ivy's house – where she had no right to be – and hearing her singing Christmas carols to that child and giggling like a child herself as she clattered around with her few bits of furniture.

They'd looked in the windows as they'd passed – not as if they were being nosy or anything – and shaken their heads at the desecration of Ivy's house.

There hadn't been even enough to furnish one room properly, Elsie thought. Elsie liked fat furniture all jostling for space. It made a real cosy home, did lots of nice pieces all squashed together. Holly Winters seemed to have only the very barest of essentials.

Holly Winters, they all agreed, had no right – no right at all – to be living in The Terrace.

'I think it's too cold tonight to go to church for Midnight Service,' Myrtle broke into the silence. 'We don't want to be struck down with pneumonia come the new year, do we?'

Hilda and Elsie shook their heads.

'I think I'll just worship with the telly, this year,' Elsie said. 'Maybe next year it won't be so bitter …'

Myrtle and Hilda nodded.

'About time I was making a move,' Elsie said, hauling herself out of her chair.

Myrtle creaked to her feet too.

They buttoned themselves into their coats, wished one another season's greetings, thanked Hilda for her festive hospitality, and made their way back to their respective houses in the icy darkness, averting their eyes from Ivy's house, where lights glowed from behind ill-fitting scarlet curtains and 'Rudolph the Red-Nosed Reindeer' was blaring out into the night.

'Orange,' Star chuckled triumphantly. 'Apple. Nits!'

'Nuts,' Holly laughed, scooping the discarded paper from Star's bed. Star didn't know it was old free-sheets. It made exciting crackling noises and revealed even more excitement when it was torn apart. 'And a bar of chocolate and packets of sweets and a tiny teddy! Hasn't Father Christmas been kind, Star? Aren't you a lucky girl?'

Star, her mouth smeared with chocolate, beamed and raised sticky hands to Holly who swept her daughter up into her arms and carried her downstairs.

It was cold in the bedrooms, but she'd got up very early and riddled the logs in the downstairs fireplace and they danced and sparked and glowed now and the living room was toastily snug. Holly opened the door.

'Oooh!' Star's eyes were enormous. 'Fairy magic!'

'Fairy magic,' Holly agreed, putting her down, watching with tenderness as she toddled towards the tree.

Of course, it wasn't a real Christmas tree, just a blown-down branch she'd found in the garden when she'd been looking for wood for the fire, but hung with the best baubles and lights the charity shop and Poundland could offer, Holly was sure it'd put Trafalgar Square to shame.

The paper chains had been a real labour of love. Strips of colourful paper cut from discarded glossy magazines and glued together, they hung and spun from the ceiling in a rainbow profusion.

'And we've got a chicken for dinner, and I've made a great big cake. Aren't we lucky?'

'Lucky ...' Star repeated, settling down on the carpet-strip in front of the fire, and staring wide-eyed at the dancing, glittering room.

It started to snow at just after two o'clock. Star rushed to the window, pointing delightedly at the fat, goose-feather flakes as they swirled faster and ever faster from the low, gunmetal sky. Holly watched too, cuddling her daughter, feeling a shiver of pure happiness. It was so perfect. She really couldn't ask for more.

'We'll build a snowman tomorrow,' she told Star. 'And throw snowballs, then maybe we could make a sledge from the tea-tray and – oh, look! There's one of our new neighbours. Wave, Star. Wave.'

Hilda, having stepped outside to brush the rapidly-accumulating snow from her doorstep, stared at the girl and the child waving through Ivy's window and shook her head. Really! Brazen little so-and-so! And now what was she doing? Opening the window! Really!

'Happy Christmas!' Holly called. 'Isn't this lovely? A white Christmas! My name's Holly and this is Star.'

Lovely? And *Star*? What a ludicrous name! The girl was absolutely mad. Hilda smiled a tight smile but because she knew her manners, muttered, 'Hilda Thornton.'

11

'Smashing to meet you.' Holly's breath hovered in smoky plumes. 'Oh, and …?'

Elsie and Myrtle, hearing voices – the first that day – had appeared on their doorsteps.

'Mrs Luscombe and Mrs Bennett,' Hilda sighed, nodding towards them. 'Myrtle and Elsie.'

They all stared at her, this girl who was living in Ivy's house, with ill-concealed suspicion.

'I suppose you're all ever so busy with your families,' Holly called along The Terrace, which was now disappearing under a glittering white cloak, 'but I mean – well, Star and I are on our own and I wondered if you'd like to come in for a minute. I've made a huge cake, far too much for us. I don't suppose you'd like to …?'

'No, I don't think so, thanks all the same,' Hilda said shortly, brushing the snowflakes from her hair and starting as she meant to go on.

Elsie took a deep breath. 'Well, actually, yes, thank you. I'd love to come in …' She stepped gingerly on to the path. 'After all, it *is* Christmas …'

And without getting her coat or gloves or sensible shoes, she walked carefully towards Ivy's house.

Myrtle and Hilda stared wordlessly at her and then at each other. Had Elsie gone *mad*?

'We're all on our own,' Elsie said defiantly, shivering in the icy snow. 'And I think a cup of tea and a slice of cake with our new neighbour would be just grand. Don't you, ladies?'

Myrtle and Hilda still started, then mumbling and grumbling – they never crossed Elsie if they could help it – they followed her unsteady trail along the terrace, the snow seeping into their slippers and settling on their perms.

'Oh! I'm so glad we're all going to be friends!' Holly opened the door wide and ushered them inside. 'Look, Star – it's like the Three Wise Men.' She grinned at Myrtle, Elsie, and Hilda. 'Star's really into the Christmas story this year. Please come in …'

They stepped inside, into warmth and colour and Christmas.

The furniture was sparse, true. There wasn't a proper carpet on the floor, and the curtains looked terrible, but logs sparked and roared in the grate, the tree sparkled in the corner, and the paper-chains danced in the draught from the front door.

'Not Three Wise Men,' Star toddled towards them, beaming. 'Three Nannas.'

Hilda, Myrtle, and Elsie looked at each other with moist eyes, then smiled happily at Star, then at Holly Winters, who had no right to be living in The Terrace, but who had turned Ivy's house into a home.

A Christmas Murder

Marsali Taylor

Three candles flickered gold above the Advent wreath of yew and holly, two red candles and one pink. It was Gaudete Sunday, where the solemnity of Advent was set aside for the joyous reading from Isaiah: *The eyes of the blind shall be opened, the deaf shall hear, the lame will leap like a stag* ... My heart sang to the words. Maman was beside me, in her sweeping white wool coat, home for Christmas. I couldn't believe it was really happening, Dad and she smiling at each other after all these years apart, but this wasn't the season to question miracles. I hugged them both at the sign of peace, and felt Father Mikhail's blessing fall on us like a promise.

My *Khalida*, the little yacht I called home, was moored in Scalloway now I was at college. The night blazed with stars as we drove through the darkness, crossing the narrow centre of Shetland's cross shape from Lerwick on the east, then became orange as we curved around the quarry into the lights of Scalloway, the old capital, on the west; seven minutes to drive from the North Sea to the Atlantic coast. We picked up my Cat, then headed north for the half-hour drive to Brae.

Maman had prepared a special dinner to celebrate her return: a glass of Pinot with twists of salmon, boar pâté on crisp biscuits, and bowls of green and black olives, followed by a roast of venison and a rich, red Morgon, then a cheese board, and finally French-style patisserie, washed down with champagne. Cat thought he'd gone to heaven. He had a good shot at wrecking

15

the Christmas tree, scoffed a plateful of venison trimmings, then curled up in front of the fire, plumed tail curled over his little nose, and purred loudly enough to be heard in Sumburgh. Dad glowed with satisfaction at having both his women under one roof at last, and Maman sang in the kitchen as she prepared each plate.

Then Maman's phone rang. We saw from her face as she recognised the caller that it was trouble, and soon realised what trouble, from her end of the conversation: a singer gone sick from a Christmas performance. 'I must ask my husband,' Maman said firmly. 'I will phone you back.'

She cut the caller off and gave Dad an indecisive look. 'It is Pierre, who gave me my first big chance. He needs someone urgently to sing Junon in *Platée*, at Chenonceau, for the three days before Christmas.'

'Well,' Dad said calmly, 'we'll have Christmas in France, Eugénie. I'll pull a string or two, see what flights I can get with BP.'

Maman's dark eyes turned to me. The moment of truth had come.

'I wasn't sure I'd be here for Christmas,' I said. 'Gavin asked me down to meet his family.'

Dad's mouth dropped open. There was a heartbeat of silence, then Maman asked smoothly, 'Gavin is who?'

My cheeks were scarlet. 'DI Gavin Macrae, from Inverness.'

Maman considered the rank and respectability. 'I think I did not meet him.'

'He wore a kilt,' Dad said. 'Nice lad,' he added to Maman. I suppressed a smile; he hadn't called him that when we'd shared the honour of being Chief Suspect.

'So,' Maman said. 'When are you going down?'

I'd been watching the charts for a fortnight. 'Probably a week today. There's a nice weather window tracking its way across the Atlantic. It's a two-day sail, with a wind on the beam.'

'You are *sailing* down, at this time of year?'

'That's why I wasn't sure about it,' I said, setting aside the belly-squirming fear of going to stay with a man I liked very much but barely knew. 'It all depends on the wind.'

'But you will freeze!'

'Not,' I said calmly, taking advantage of being the restored prodigal, 'if you get me a new Musto mid-layer suit for Christmas.'

Maman's mouth opened again. Dad's hand came up to her arm. 'We'll see you here for the New Year.'

They both came to drive me home: through the darkness of the Kames, past the moonlight glinting on Tingwall Loch, around the curve, and down towards the seafront. It was getting on for midnight.

'*Tiens*,' Maman said. 'There is a *Père Noël* on the roof of your castle.'

Dad swerved to look. 'So there is. Wonder how they got him up there.'

He was up on the wall-top of Earl Patrick's ruined castle, a stuffed figure dressed in Santy's scarlet hat, breeks, and jacket, with a black belt and bearded false-face. A sheet flapping from the gable said 'HO HO HO!' in spray-painted letters. We had a glimpse, then he was hidden behind roofs as Dad headed for Port Arthur.

I pondered the 'who' as I put the hot water bottle in my bed and brushed my teeth on deck. I could make a guess. I'd been worried that I'd lose my head for mast-climbing with all this time ashore, so I'd taken to going along to the climbing wall at Clickimin, the leisure centre in Lerwick – and it just so happened that two of the Climbing Club members lived right here in Scalloway. One of them was called Derek, and he lived in one of the New Street houses. He was a doctor in Lerwick, and I suspected half his surgery was silly women inventing ailments just to see him, because he was stunningly handsome in that broad-shouldered, blond-haired way. They needn't have bothered; I regularly saw him with his wife and their troupe of golden-haired children in the shop, at the park, or just walking along the seafront, looking like a devoted family unit.

The other one, Ertie, lived along the Port Arthur road. He, Derek, and Derek's wife had been students together in Aberdeen, fifteen years ago. Now he was a maths teacher, a cheery soul with brown hair and eyes. His wide grin revealed capped front teeth, a souvenir of a particularly rough rugby game. He'd kept a student sense of humour, and putting Santy on Scalloway Castle would have been right up his street.

It was a fair height though, and I wouldn't have

cared to tackle the climb up with a dummy on my back. Much easier to have two of you, and haul it up once you'd reached the top. It was a two-person sort of fun, with secret planning phone calls beforehand, and stifled giggles and glances across at still-lit windows in the houses of Castle Street as you manhandled the dummy across the road. Now, what was the name of that dark-haired girl who hung around with the two of them? Janette … no, Janine. She was a secretary somewhere in town, pretty, and a competent climber. I'd got the impression she was single, so she'd be available for jolly japes in the run-up to Christmas, unlike Derek, who'd be busy worrying about preparations for children's stockings and in-laws for lunch.

I fished out my mobile and sent a text to Ertie: *Ho ho ho 2 u 2*, then wormed into my berth, curled over to let Cat settle into the crook of my neck, and slept.

I was heating my lunchtime soup when I heard something bumping against *Khalida*'s hull. It sounded sizeable but soft, a dead seal or porpoise maybe. I grimaced, hauled my oilskin jacket on and came out through the washboards.

It had been a clear, cold morning, as the starry night had promised, with the sun glittering on the sea. The tide had come in till midday, and was retreating again now. The bumping object had caught at the corner of the *Khalida*'s berth on its way seawards. I felt my heart stop, then start again, thumping as if it wanted to push its way out of my breast. For a moment I'd thought – but it was just a Guy Fawkes dummy, a navy

19

boiler suit with knotted sleeves and trousers, stuffed to bursting with straw, and with a grey float for a head. It hadn't been long in the water, for the straw wasn't sodden enough to sink – dumped on the shore, maybe, after high water yesterday, and taken off by this morning's tide.

Then I remembered the season. Guy Fawkes was long past. Yesterday, people were getting into panic mode about last posting dates for Christmas, and whether Shetland Transport would deliver the parcels from south in time; and high water had been at eleven at night. Only one joker was doing dummies at that hour.

I turned to face the castle, tall and grim against the green hill. The splash of scarlet was huddled in the angle between gable and chimney stack, beside the white rectangle with its black writing. I reached into *Khalida*'s cabin for my spy-glasses. The castle sprang up, each stone shadow-sharp. I moved my field of vision up to the gable, and found the scarlet figure. Now I could see that the black belt was a cord doubled around his waist, holding him in place. He didn't have that stiff-armed look a straw dummy has, and there was a seagull perched on his shoulder, pecking sideways under the false face. I lowered the binoculars, feeling sick, then reached for my mobile.

College hadn't yet closed for Christmas. It was hard to concentrate on the Region B buoyage system when I was wondering what was going on over at the castle. They'd have to get the body down. Even with all the rules about not touching a crime scene, they couldn't just leave it there for the gulls, in full sight of all Scalloway. Easiest, I supposed, would be to get helicopter Oscar Charlie in, and have the winchman untie it and lower it to the ground. I didn't envy him the job.

How had the murderer got the body up there? Now we were talking serious climbing skills, the ability to rig a working pulley and use it up at that height to haul a dead-weight body. Ertie certainly would be able; probably Derek too. Janine would have the skills, but she was my height and build, and I wasn't sure I would have the strength.

And what a public place to be messing around with a dead body! I wondered, between looking at the whiteboard and writing lists of countries, how long it would take. You'd have to go up, fix the pulley, go back down for the rope – no, you could attach the body, then take the pulley and rope up.

No, more simply, you could do it from inside. A fireman's lift to the first floor Great Hall, then up the inside, and haul your body in peace without and fear of being seen. Place him, tie him, shimmy down again. I wondered who had access to the castle keys?

Most importantly, *who was it*?

'Derek Broadhurst,' DI Gavin Macrae from Inverness told me, two days later, in *Khalida*'s cabin,

He was wearing his dress tartan, in honour of the season, with a Cairngorm the yellow of Cat's eyes twinkling in the silver hilt of the dagger in his stocking. He shut the washboards behind him, then sat down on the other side of the little prop-leg table in a swirl of scarlet pleats. His hair gleamed russet in the candle-light.

'I don't expect there were any,' I said. I'd been psyching myself up to meet him off-duty on his own ground, so it was disconcerting to have him suddenly here again in *Khalida's* cabin. I poured him a glass of the boat's emergency whisky. He sniffed it doubtfully.

'Are you trying to keep the cold out?'

'It can get a bit chilly,' I admitted. I put Cat to the floor and set the kettle on the gas cooker. 'But the gas ring soon warms it up, once you get it going. So, tell me more.'

'I was hoping you'd tell me. Dr Broadhurst, married, four children under eight, lives in Scalloway, practice in Lerwick. A ladies' man?'

'He was charming,' I conceded, 'but you never saw him out without his family.'

'Natural charm, or calculated?'

I considered that one. 'Natural, I'd say. He even smarmed me a bit, and the professional womanizers don't usually bother. What does his practice say?'

'His fellow doctors were certain there was no trouble with patients. One of them conceded he might have strayed outside his marriage from time to time. The practice secretary was less discreet, even a touch embittered – she reckoned he had a girlfriend on the go most of the time.'

I pictured his wife, trim and immaculate, and always smiling. 'Did his wife know?'

Gavin wrinkled his nose. 'She seemed less surprised than I'd expect at his going out for a walk so late at night, and it was you who reported the body. She didn't report him missing – not even the next morning.'

'Nothing from the weapon?' I'd been in a classroom that faced out to sea when the body had been taken down, but I'd heard all about it from the owner of the house opposite, an old lady who was over ninety, with good eyesight, good spy-glasses, and a gossip chain Miss Marple would envy. It had been a knife to the heart, she'd told me: 'A straight thrust, like a doctor had made it.'

'A thin, sharp blade,' Gavin said, 'like a surgical knife, thrust efficiently in the right place. It was taken away, but if we find it we'll be able to match it to the wound.'

'And how about how he got up there? A ladder, or one of those lift things?'

Gavin shook his head. 'It's too high for a ladder.'

'Even from the inside?'

'It would be hard, even with two of you, to get a long enough ladder up the stairs, and I'm never keen on the two-people theory for a murder.'

'One of those truck things, with the pulpit on a ladder?'

'No. The lady opposite was semi-awake most of the night, dealing with a child who'd eaten too many sweeties at a party on Sunday afternoon. She's certain she'd have heard even a car stopping, let alone a cherry-picker. However, she did see two people, both

23

dressed as Santa, just past the castle. One was supporting the other, as if he was drunk. She couldn't tell the time exactly, but after eleven, and she couldn't say what they looked like – well, they looked like Santa, and she wasn't surprised to see him about at this season.'

'So it sounds like the person responsible was a doctor, who could climb.' I didn't want to think it was Ertie, but I wondered if he'd done any medical training – been a member of a mountain rescue team, say.

'Yes; such a pity the prime candidate's also the victim.' Gavin drank his whisky gloomily, and rose. 'I've done all I can do for this evening.' He paused in the doorway, suddenly awkward. 'Are you still thinking to come down for Christmas?'

I nodded. 'The weekend's looking hopeful.'

'Good.' He nodded goodbye and headed off.

It was the next morning before I remembered the dummy. Gavin didn't need two murderers, just one. Derek had climbed up there under his own steam, with the dummy and – someone else. They'd planned the Santa joke together, dressed as Santa themselves to make it more fun, and to hide who they were in case someone else saw them, set up the sheet (a two-man job that, I remembered the way it had flapped in the wind) then the someone else had stabbed him, tied him up, and come down with the dummy. He or she had staggered down to the Burn beach with it, just as the lady in the house had seen them, taken the scarlet

Santa suit off, and thrown the dummy over for the water to take away.

I wondered, I just wondered, if Derek's wife had also learned to climb in their student days.

There were fewer people on the climbing wall that evening. I wasn't sure if it was tact, or just pre-Christmas engagements. I was almost at the top of the 'hardest' route when Ertie came up beside me. 'Now then,' he said.

'Now,' I replied, gave myself a last push to the top, got my toehold, scrambled, turned, and sat on an iron beam of Clickimin's roof. Now I was as high as the first platform of *Sorlandet*'s mast. I looped my harness around the beam, and let my legs dangle. Below me, behind a net, two pairs of badminton players rushed about like human spiders. The 'thwack' as each hit echoed around the metal ceiling.

Ertie came up to join me. He sat for a moment, watching the badminton, then sighed. 'I don't believe it.'

'I saw him on the roof late on Sunday,' I said. 'I thought it was a joke.' I glanced sideways at his set jaw. 'I thought it was you, actually – that had done it, I mean, when I thought it was a dummy.'

He grimaced. 'I wish now I had joined in. Maybe, then, he'd still be alive. But I don't understand –'

'Hang on,' I said, 'you mean you knew about it?'

'I was there when they discussed it. In the pub, after a session. Someone said what a good fun it would be, and Derek agreed.'

'It wasn't his idea, then?'

'No.' Ertie frowned, remembering. 'No, I think it was Janine's.' He looked around, as if expecting to see her. 'Of course, she'd not be here today. The whole practice is devastated.'

My head jerked up. 'I thought she was a secretary.'

'She is – to Derek's practice.'

'Access to the weapon,' I told Gavin, after the arrest. 'Medical knowledge. A climber. She had it all planned.'

'Once we looked it wasn't hard to get evidence. The neighbour identified his photo as her boyfriend. Funny the neighbour didn't recognise him.'

'The east-west divide,' I said. 'He was Scalloway. He socialised and shopped there, not in Lerwick. Conversely, she never came over to Scalloway, and so never saw him with the family.'

'Janine thought he'd leave his wife – until she saw them all Christmas shopping in Commercial Street.' All together, looking like a united family. Like Maman and Dad on Gaudete Sunday, after all these years apart. Sometimes the first bonds were the strongest. 'Then she got angry. For two years, he'd strung her along … There was a knife missing from his consulting room.'

'In the sea, probably.'

'She had a ticket for yesterday's boat. If you hadn't found that dummy she'd have been gone before anyone looked closer at the body on the Castle.'

'That was where her planning let her down,' I said.

26

'The east-west divide. I bet she'd looked it up, so that she threw it in at high tide, so the sea would take it away.'

'But it didn't,' Gavin said.

'No,' I agreed. 'She'd looked up the Lerwick tide tables. High water Lerwick was at one o'clock. The Atlantic tide on the west side is two hours earlier.'

I set down my mug and looked at my watch. 'Watch the time for your flight.'

Gavin grimaced and rose. 'So … let me know when you set out. Safe journey.'

'See you in Scotland,' I said.

Santa Lives

Tricia Maw

I know the local launderette isn't an ideal place to spend Christmas Eve, but it sure beats my empty house.

I'd dropped the two boys off at their father's earlier in the day. It was Martin's turn to have them for Christmas this year, an amicable arrangement which usually suits all of us, but after I'd left I was full of nervous energy. Louisa, Martin's new wife, has that effect on me. She'd strolled down the stairs in a black, skin-tight jumpsuit looking immaculately groomed and impossibly thin. Don't get me wrong, I don't resent Louisa and I'm certainly not jealous of her. She's really good for Martin and the children think she's cool. But sometimes, she makes me feel fat, frumpy, and middle-aged.

Consequently, I arrived home in a bad mood, already regretting turning down an invitation to spend Christmas with friends. I decided to work off my bad temper by having a blitz on the kids' bedrooms, something I'd put off for too long. By the time I'd finished and shoved the duvets into the car it was almost dark and the launderette was empty and hot. I sat round the corner by the dryers and picked up a magazine. It was quiet and peaceful and the gentle sloshing noise of the machines made my eyes feel heavy.

I must have dozed off because, when I looked at the washing machine opposite me, I could see Santa Claus rolling around inside. His fat red trousers, his matching jacket trimmed with fur, and his long, white whiskers were pressed up against the glass, trying to get out.

'Oh, you poor man!' I cried. 'Let me help you.' I rushed towards the machine just as a large dark shape appeared at the launderette's glass door. Pinching myself to make sure I was awake, I looked at the shape again. It was definitely Santa's reindeer. Snow covered its fur, its antlers tapped against the door, and its breath misted the glass.

'I don't need any help,' a voice said behind me. 'I'm OK. Please don't turn round.'

I turned round. A naked man, looking very embarrassed, tried not to meet my eyes. I opened my mouth to scream. Well, you do hear of strange goings-on in launderettes.

Then a dog barked.

'Be quiet, Bonzo,' the naked man said. 'He thinks you're going to attack me,' he added apologetically.

Bonzo? I looked at the reindeer which was standing on its hind legs pawing at the glass. It was definitely a dog.

'I thought …' I stopped. I wasn't quite sure what I thought any more. I looked closely at the man and realised he wasn't entirely naked. He was wearing a rather snazzy pair of red and white striped boxer shorts and a large pair of black boots. On the bench beside him was a brass bell.

'You're Father Christmas,' I said accusingly.

He nodded sheepishly. 'Gerry Drysdale, actually.' He smiled disarmingly and held out his hand.

'Tessa Stanton.' I put my hand in his.

Bonzo chose that moment to put both paws on the

door handle and bound into the room. Leaping excitedly, he shook snow over both of us. We stepped out of his way as the antlers slipped over his eyes and he crashed into the washing machine. One of its knobs flew off and rolled across the floor out of sight. The machine gave a protesting gurgle and stopped in mid-cycle.

I hate to admit it but I got a fit of the giggles. Gerry's face was a picture of horror when he realised the machine was jammed with his clothes still inside and neither of us could get it to start again.

'I was only doing this as a favour for my dad,' he wailed. 'He's been Santa Claus at Barton's department store since he retired, but he wasn't feeling well last week and asked if I'd stand in for him. Then, one of the little darlings threw up all over the suit, so I nipped into the launderette to wash it. I didn't think there'd be anyone here.' It was his turn to sound accusing.

I took pity on him and threw him a quilt cover out of the dryer. 'Here, wrap this round you and I'll drive you home.'

Later that evening the house didn't seem empty any more. Bonzo, minus his antlers, was asleep in front of the fire. Gerry, wearing a pair of Martin's old gardening trousers and a shirt I'd found at the back of the airing cupboard, was stretched out on the couch.

I thought of Louisa, having to cope with my two boisterous children and hating every minute of it, and felt full of joy and goodwill. Gerry was cooking Christmas dinner for his dad tomorrow and that was one invitation I didn't turn down.

I put my hand in the pocket of my jeans and curled my fingers round the washing machine knob. I didn't feel the slightest bit guilty. After all, I told myself, it isn't every day you meet Santa Claus in the launderette.

No Smoke Without Fire

Bill Kitson

It was the pre-Christmas meeting of the three emergency services. It was held at Dinsdale police headquarters, as was customary, following a series of tragic events surrounding past festive seasons. Their focus was to ensure their response was as efficient as possible, should similar circumstances arise.

Detective Sergeant Lucas Sharp, known as Luke, had only been transferred to Dinsdale a few months earlier, and most of the names and faces were unfamiliar to him. Seated alongside Luke was another newcomer, Dr Paula Morton, who would be the emergency doctor on duty throughout the festivities. Introducing themselves before the formalities, they agreed that having arrived recently meant they had both been handed the short straw.

They listened as Detective Superintendent Geoff Parker outlined the reason they were there. 'It seems that the festive season attracts the worst kind of behaviour, whether irresponsible or malicious. In the last few years this has been marked by three major incidents, all of them tragic in their own way, and two of them linked.' He glanced down at the notes in front of him. 'Ten years ago, on Christmas Eve, Towlers department store was robbed. Soon after the staff left the premises, two armed, masked men forced their way into the building, overpowered the security guards, bound and gagged them, broke open the safe in the manager's office, and escaped with the takings. What started as an armed robbery became even more serious because one of the security men suffered a heart attack and died.'

Parker paused for emphasis. 'The intruders were never apprehended. Suspicion fell on two local lowlifes, but there was insufficient evidence to bring a prosecution. The surviving security guard was arrested, and when his house was searched, officers discovered a cache of money amounting to several thousand pounds. He protested his innocence, claiming that he had won the money on a day's outing to Wetherby races. He said he was saving it to surprise his wife and children at Christmas with a holiday to Disneyland Florida. Although there was evidence that he did attend that race meeting, the jury did not believe his story.'

Parker glanced at his audience and could tell they didn't believe the tale either. 'The security guard, whose name was Danny Butler, was sentenced to fifteen years, with manslaughter being added to the conspiracy and armed robbery charges.'

If those hardened by their profession had been unmoved by the superintendent's account, this was certainly not the case when he invited an officer from the traffic division to describe the second tragedy.

'It was three years ago. There had been little snow, but in the weeks leading up to Christmas, the temperatures were sub-zero. Despite the best efforts of the local authority, many of the minor routes in the dale were highly treacherous due to black ice. The road leading to the summit of Black Fell was one of the worst affected. A few days before Christmas, a convoy of vehicles set out on this road to attend a party at Dinsdale Hall Hotel, close to the summit. As they negotiated a hairpin bend, we believe one of the cars skidded on the ice and collided with another causing a chain reaction.'

He looked at his audience, his face grim as he continued. 'All three cars went over the edge and down a two-hundred-foot drop. Fire destroyed the vehicles, killing the occupants. Seven people lost their lives. It is by far the worst RTA this area has ever suffered.'

Having heard this harrowing account, the senior paramedic added, 'We have the task of responding to these incidents and the effect on all concerned is traumatic, not only for those involved but also for those attending. And our time is also wasted out on the streets, picking up members of the public who are celebrating the season, not only at the time but for weeks ahead. Our resources could be far better utilised.'

Geoff Parker nodded in agreement and turned to the Chief Fire Officer who stood up before continuing. 'Last Christmas Eve, a fire destroyed a house on the Normanton estate. There were three people in the building, a mother and her two children. All three died of smoke inhalation. The cause of the fire was later determined as arson. Petrol had been poured through the letterbox and ignited.'

Parker took over the commentary. 'Remember I said two of the events were linked? The three who were killed in the fire were Danny Butler's wife

Sandra plus their two children. I had the unenviable task of driving out to Felling Prison and telling Butler the news. I have to say, I pity the people responsible for that fire should Butler ever catch up with them.'

Luke Sharp interrupted, speaking for the first time. 'You made one connection between the events, Geoff, is there any chance the fire might have been some form of reprisal aimed at Butler?'

'Good question, and the answer is we simply don't know. We can't even be sure there was a motive, as such. It might have simply been the random act of a psychopath. Fortunately, there have been no further incidents of that kind.'

Parker looked round to see if there were any further questions. Everyone seemed preoccupied, dwelling on the senseless waste of so many lives. 'You can appreciate why we need to be totally prepared. The plans we put together in this meeting could literally be life or death decisions. We have to bear in mind that it is not only the public, but also our colleagues, that we have to protect.'

When the meeting ended, Luke Sharp turned to Paula Morton. 'I don't know about you, Doctor, but I could do with a pint.'

'I'm with you there. Listening to your boss and the others was a bit like reading one of the gorier plots by that bloke who writes thrillers set round here.' She smiled. 'Lead me to the nearest bar.'

They walked across Dinsdale's market square, which was almost deserted in the early evening despite the fact that it had been market day. The only people in sight were council workmen who were dismantling the stalls, and their colleagues who were cleaning up the litter that was the inevitable result of the day's activity.

The town was shrouded in fog. For once, it seemed that the weather forecasters had got it right, as Sharp commented. 'At least we won't have to contend with black ice this year, the forecast is for mild, foggy weather until Christmas.'

They entered the Three Tuns Hotel and headed for the bar, where Luke asked her what she wanted to drink. Much to his surprise, Paula asked for a pint of Theakston's. He ordered two pints of bitter. As they took their seats in the bay window, Paula noticed that Luke opted for the one in the corner. She wondered if that was to hide the ugly purple birthmark that covered one side of his face. He asked for Paula's opinion of the meeting they had just left.

'It would have depressed me had I been that way inclined, but as a doctor I'm used to having to deal with things that have already taken their toll. The number of times where we can be proactive in prevention, rather than attempting a cure, is sadly not enough.'

'We're much the same. Crime prevention is only a small part of our work, and when things like that arson attack happen, we have no chance of stopping them. It makes you feel so helpless.'

'If you were to find the person responsible, would that be classed as murder?'

'You'd think so, wouldn't you? But some smart defence barrister would probably argue the case. The difficulty would be proving the intent was to kill those inside rather than simply torch the building. However, from what Geoff Parker said, it sounds like a hypothetical question. After all this time, we stand little chance of identifying the perpetrator, short of a miracle.'

Paula smiled sympathetically. 'You never know, Luke. It'll be Christmas soon, and that's supposed to be the season of miracles.'

'You may be right, should we cross our fingers or something?'

They laughed, took a drink, and looked round at the bar which was beginning to fill. 'How are you settling in to the area?' Paula asked.

'I haven't had much time to get to know anyone around here, so it's a bit of a relief being on duty over Christmas. Otherwise I'd be bored out of my mind.'

'Don't you have family to go to?'

Sharp shook his head. 'No family, not of my own at least.' He looked at Paula and decided she was the understanding sort. He added, 'I was abandoned as a baby by my mother, raised by foster parent after foster parent for years.'

'That must have been hard for you. Were you never adopted? Surely there was a lot of demand for babies and toddlers?'

Paula was surprised by the grim expression on Sharp's face. His reply was given with great reluctance, it seemed, 'I believe so, but as someone from the adoption service kindly told me, nobody wants to take responsibility for a child with deformities such as mine.'

If she'd been surprised earlier, Paula was shocked by the bitterness in Sharp's voice. 'What deformities? I can see you have a birthmark, but lots of people have them. Not all as visible, maybe.' She winced at her own tactlessness.

'That's not the one I was referring to. I was born with one leg shorter than the other. It caused a very ungainly limp, which put people off. Naturally, those who saw me before I could walk had to think up other excuses to reject me.'

'There's no trace of it now.'

'No, I had to go to America for a very expensive operation which helped. I also wear hand-made shoes that correct the remaining imbalance. There's no trace of a limp unless I get really tired.'

'Were you were adopted eventually, then?'

'Yes, but not until I was almost twelve years old. That's why I became a police officer. It was a policeman and his wife who finally took pity on me.'

'Via the adoption agency, I presume?'

'No, the officer caught me about to help myself to some sweets in a local shop. He was off duty, and instead of having me arrested he talked to me, found out my history, and a couple of days later he brought his wife to meet me at the foster home.'

'What persuaded them to adopt you?'

Sharp's habitually dour expression lightened a little. 'The sweets I was trying to steal were toffees

40

which I'd never had. He couldn't understand how a child could reach my age without ever having tasted a toffee. Then I told him nobody had ever bought me sweets. The only ones I'd ever had were ones I'd stolen.'

'They must be like a family to you, surely?'

'Oh, they are, but this year they're in Australia visiting my older sister, their daughter, and her family. I can't begrudge them that. They gave me everything I have, including my job.'

'How do you mean?'

'By the time I was old enough, my adoptive father had been promoted. He wangled me into the force, even though the medical wasn't encouraging.'

'He must have a fair amount of influence to do that.'

'You could say that.' Luke laughed as he took a drink. 'He's a deputy chief constable.'

'Oh, I see. And you've never married? Don't you miss having a family of your own at this time of year?' Paula realised she was being tactless again.

He dismissed the question with a shake of his head. 'Never found the right girl.' Then he laughed again, 'But there are advantages. I don't have to buy a load of expensive presents. Anyway, enough about me. How about you? Are your family local?'

'Hardly,' Paula smiled. 'My parents are retired. They live in Spain. My sister works in New York, and my brother's in London.'

'So you'll be on your own too over Christmas. Perhaps we could get together for a drink?'

Was that a subtle way of asking for a date? Paula wondered. No, somehow that didn't seem like him. Luke seemed too reserved to do anything so bold.

Before she left, they swapped phone numbers. Luke watched her go with regret. He liked Paula, and if he'd been more self-confident, he might have asked her out. It had been easy talking to her. Even mentioning his deformities hadn't seemed to put her off. Or perhaps she was just being kind. That reservation was always at the back of his mind. Despite his many qualities, despite his successful career, Luke was unable to accept that people could like him for who he was and ignore his physical defects.

As Christmas drew nearer, there was no relief from the oppressive fog that had settled like a blanket on the dale. By the late afternoon of Christmas Eve, as shoppers struggled from shop to shop, attempting to beat the closing deadline, several minor accidents had caused traffic chaos. Taking advantage of their near-invisibility, thieves had gone on a shoplifting, mugging, and pickpocketing spree.

On the Normanton council estate on the outskirts of Dinsdale, Lauren stared out of the window. She hated the fog, detested the clammy, damp weather. The way people loomed out of the swirling mist frightened her, always had. She would have liked to have been out in the open air, but dare not go in weather like this. Staying indoors was marginally preferable, even though it meant she had to contend with her stepfather, who she hated even more than the fog. Not that Terry was her stepfather, not officially at least. He was just living with Lauren's mother.

If she had to list the things she disliked about Terry, Lauren would have struggled to know where to start. She would probably have opted for the way he treated her mother, or the money he spent on booze and drugs. There again, it would more likely have been his friendship with Wayne.

No matter how she mistrusted Terry, or how disturbed she was by the way he looked at her sometimes, Lauren's feelings about Terry paled into insignificance compared to those she had about Wayne. She not only hated him, she was scared of him. Wayne had made no attempt to disguise what he would like to do to her, and had even tried to put the threat into effect on one occasion, but luckily, Lauren had been able to avoid him.

On Christmas Eve, her mother had been at work until lunchtime and had only been back in the house half an hour, having done all the shopping, when she received a text. She walked into the lounge, where Lauren was adding Christmas cards to the display she'd carefully made. Terry was sprawled in an armchair watching an old film on TV.

'I've had a message from work,' she announced. 'Apparently they've had some problem reconciling the takings and they want me to go back in. It might take a while. Sorry, about this, but I don't have any choice. I should be home in time for dinner.' She smiled at Lauren. 'That looks very nice; in fact everything you've done in here is lovely.' She admired the tidy room with the decorated tree in the corner and the streamers hanging from the ceiling. 'Will you turn the oven on later if I'm not back?' she asked, as she struggled in to her coat.

'No problem, Mum.'

No sooner had she left when Terry's mobile bleeped. He scanned the message, before telling Lauren, 'Wayne's coming over and bringing some beer with him. You be nice to him, you hear me? He might even give you a Christmas present.' He laughed at her expression.

Lauren's heart sank. She guessed that it wouldn't only be beer Wayne brought. He'd also bring drugs. And that could spell trouble. With her mother out, she would be trapped inside the house with those two. She racked her brains trying to think of some excuse to go out, or someone she could visit, but without success.

Wayne was in the pub. The Red Lion was by no means the most salubrious drinking establishment in Dinsdale, but the management had a relaxed attitude to what went on under their roof. This suited Wayne and many others. If not all the drinkers were old enough in the eyes of the law it didn't matter, as long as their money was good. And if some of the customers wanted to do a little trading in substances frowned on by the authorities during their visits to the pub, so what? It would have been counter-productive to ban this, or ask them not to, for fear of losing their lucrative trade. Wayne had been in the pub since lunchtime. Although by no means drunk, he was far from completely sober by the time his mobile beeped with an incoming message.

He read the text with interest, and then re-read it with mounting excitement. 'M out til late. Can u cum over n bring beer and gear. L says she want u to cum! T'

Wayne looked round the bar, and saw the barman was not busy. Ten minutes later, armed with a couple of six-packs, he left the pub. He set off walking towards the estate, but first he had a call to make. He hoped that visiting the allotment on Christmas Eve wouldn't arouse anyone's suspicions. If so, he'd have to claim he was getting sprouts for the Christmas dinner. Having said that, he doubted if even the most suspicious copper would think of an allotment shed as a likely hiding place for drugs. Wayne smiled happily. Sinking some beers and smoking some weed was fine, but if he got really lucky, he might get his leg over too. Fancy Lauren wanting to see him. She'd never shown any interest before. The fact that Lauren was only fourteen didn't worry him.

Lauren's mother had been gone little more than half an hour when the doorbell rang. It was Wayne, and Lauren could tell he had been drinking. As soon as they were seated in the lounge, Wayne opened a can and passed a second one to Terry. 'I'll stand the beers,' he said generously. 'I got the weed from the shed, like you asked.'

'What weed?'

'The gear you asked me to bring.'

'I didn't ask you for any gear. Still, as you've got

45

some, it'd be a shame to waste it.'

'Hang on, Tel. You said I had to bring some gear.'

'I never said anything of the sort. You told me you'd bring the beer and the gear.'

'When did I say that?'

'In your text. "I'll bring beer and gear" you said.'

'I never. Your text said "bring beer and gear".'

'What text? I didn't send you a text. You sent me one.'

'No I didn't. I was in the Red Lion and my mobile went off. That was when I read your text.'

Both men reached for their mobiles and looked at the messages. Terry reacted first. 'That's funny, there's no message from you here. I must have deleted it.'

Wayne was equally baffled. 'There's nothing on mine either, and yet I remember reading it. There's something weird going on.'

'Still, doesn't matter, does it. Might as well enjoy ourselves, eh? It's Christmas, after all.'

Somehow, in the process of getting themselves geared up, as Wayne referred to it, he ended up seated alongside Lauren on the sofa. This was absolutely the last thing she wanted. It was too late now for her to retire to the privacy of her own room. That would be seen as an insult to Terry's guest, and the repercussions would be unpleasant for her. In addition, the last place she wanted to be when Wayne was in an amorous mood was a room with a bed in it. A room, moreover, where his advances could be conducted in privacy.

The next half hour was a torment for Lauren. Whenever he thought Terry wasn't watching, which was far too often for Lauren's liking, Wayne's questing hands would stroke her leg, her thigh, her breast, anywhere he could reach. She lost count of the number of times she slapped his hand, or removed it from where he had placed it. Trying to glare at him without Terry seeing her reaction.

Far from being discouraged by these small rejections, Wayne seemed to regard them as some form of foreplay. Lauren was sickened by him, his wandering hands, the whispered suggestions, and when she heard the doorbell ring again, she leapt to her feet to answer it. 'I'll go; it wouldn't do for you to find a policeman on the doorstep when you've got a joint in your mouth.'

She closed the lounge door behind her and as she walked across the hallway, had a frightening thought. What if the caller was another of Terry's mates? The last thing she wanted was yet another boozy, drug taking loser who thought he was God's gift.

She opened the front door and peered out. For a moment, such was the density of the fog that she thought there was no one in front of her. Then he stepped closer, and Lauren's eyes opened wide with surprise. It was no wonder she hadn't spotted him immediately, she thought. The caller was a complete stranger, and strange certainly fitted his appearance. He was pale, beyond what was normal. He was a little under six feet tall, dressed in light coloured clothes.

His hair was ash-blond, as were his eyebrows. His eyes were pale too, a washed-out blue that was almost opaque. There was no vestige of colour in his cheeks, save for a vivid red scar that ran from just below his left eye almost to his jaw. Lauren, who had recently seen *The Da Vinci Code,* was reminded of the albino assassin Silas.

'Can I help you?' she asked. Somehow, despite his odd appearance, the stranger didn't seem at all frightening. Not until he spoke. Then, it was what he said rather than his tone that she found bewildering and disturbing. A slight shiver ran down her spine.

'Hello, Lauren. I hope Wayne hasn't harmed you? He isn't a nice man; neither of them are.' He indicated indoors as he spoke. 'A pair of low-life scum. I didn't mean for you to have to put up with Wayne pestering you when I arranged all this.'

'What do you mean? Who are you? What do you want?' Lauren recoiled a little, unsure whether she should slam the door.

'I want you to listen. Listen and remember what happens. Because you're going to be my witness, when it's all over.'

'After what is all over?' She felt a frisson of fear.

'Wait and see. I promise you, you're safe. I will not allow anything to harm you. Is that clear?' He looked at her intently.

Lauren stared back, unable to avert her gaze from those pale eyes. She believed him, believed every word he told her. But why? Lauren was as disbelieving as most teenagers, particularly regarding what adults said. 'Yes, perfectly clear,' she replied, her words slow and measured, as if she was under the influence of that hypnotic stare.

'Now, let's go and join the others?' He smiled cheerfully. 'They should be about ready for us by now. We have to get everything done before your mother returns. The little diversion I organised for her at work won't take her too long to deal with. I think we've got about an hour, no more, but that should be enough.'

'What are you going to do?' It was curious, but despite his odd manner and his even stranger words, Lauren didn't fear this man now.

'You'll see very soon. One thing I promise you, when this is all over, you won't be troubled by either of those two again. Do you know what they're planning at this moment?'

Lauren shook her head. She wasn't sure she wanted to know, but she couldn't work out how the weird visitor could tell. Perhaps he had super-sensitive hearing. Or was he making it all up?

'I'm not sure you'll want to know, but perhaps it will ease your conscience afterwards if you realize what a narrow escape you had. As we speak, Wayne and that so-called stepfather of yours are planning a gang bang – with you. Like I said, they're a pair of loathsome creatures. You'll be better off when they're out of your life. As will your mother, for that matter. Come on, let's get it over with.'

He grasped her arm gently, and turned her to face the lounge. Although his touch was lit, when Lauren looked at her arm afterwards, she was shocked to see that it was bruised, the marks clearly defined as a hand print.

She opened the lounge door, the stranger close behind her. Both men were lolling in their seats, the effects of the drugs and beer had obviously taken their toll. They looked towards Lauren and then past her. She saw vague signs of recognition in their faces, but neither man spoke. The visitor strode past her and stooped over Terry, staring into his eyes. Terry sat up in his chair, as if at some unspoken command. Satisfied, the stranger turned and did the same to Wayne with similar results.

As he had passed her, Lauren had noticed a faint aroma, one she could not immediately place. It was only later that she recognized it. For the moment, her attention was claimed by the visitor's actions. He turned to her and asked, 'If you had a Christmas wish, Lauren, what would happen to these two?' He indicated the men, who were staring at him like adoring dogs, awaiting a command from their master.

'I wish they would disappear from out of my life and my mum's forever, but I suppose that's asking too much.' Lauren wasn't sure why she said that, it seemed right, after what she'd just gone through with Wayne, and felt it was what the stranger wanted her to say.

'I don't think it is asking too much. This is Christmas, after all, and if you can't ask for what you really want at this time of the year, when can you? Now, we have to get down to business. Are you ready?'

She nodded, her eyes fixed on his. 'And you know that you have to take careful note of everything these two say, so that you will be able to repeat it word for word to others later?'

'I do.' As she said it, Lauren thought that it sounded like a vow; which seemed ridiculous. The visitor obviously didn't think so, for he smiled encouragingly.

He turned to the two men, whose eyes were still fixed on him. 'OK, you two are going to tell Lauren everything. Everything, do you understand?'

Both men nodded, as if some invisible string was causing the heads to move in unison.

'Right, I want you to go back in time. It is Christmas Eve, ten years ago. The time is seven o'clock in the evening. Tell us what's happening, Terry.'

Terry began to speak without hesitation. 'OK, we're here, Wayne. Let's see if Arnie has left the door unlocked. Yeah, he has, but we've to make it look as if it was forced. Pass me the jemmy.'

He got to his feet and reached out a hand to grasp the imaginary tool and began levering at an unseen object. 'OK, remember what Arnie said. He's going to walk down this corridor and we pretend to nab him. We take him back to the security office, make like we're threatening him with the knife, and get the other bloke. After we knock the second guard out, we tie him up and then Arnie. Then I deal with the safe while you stand guard. What's the other one's name again? That's it, Danny. He knows nothing, so if he looks like coming round, hit him again. We can't risk letting him

51

see that Arnie's in on it.'

There was a period of silence as Terry mimed a series of actions, watched impassively by the stranger, and with open-mouthed astonishment by Lauren. Some moments later, his voice threatening, his words even more so. 'Sit still, put your hands behind your back, and don't touch anything or I'll slit your mate's throat.' As he spoke, Terry held an invisible knife horizontally in front of him.

'OK, tie him up and gag him.' He waited for what seemed an age. 'Good, now knock him out.'

Another pause, then, 'OK, he's out of it. Come on, Arnie. Let's see what Towlers have taken today. I bet this'll be your best ever Christmas bonus, eh? You all right, Arnie? You look a bit flushed – excitement getting a bit much? Wayne, remember what I told you. First sign that Danny boy there shows of waking up, you hit him good and hard.'

There was another, longer period of silence as Terry performed a series of mimes, actions that Lauren could not even begin to guess at. Eventually, he put his hands to his ears and waited, as if expecting a loud noise. He removed them, and began dusting imaginary residue from his clothing before he spoke again, his voice a hushed whisper. 'Hell's bells, Arnie, looks like we've hit the jackpot this time. Anyway, no time to count it now, we'd better tie you up, then scarper. Someone might have heard that bang and come snooping.'

Then Terry asked, 'Any problems, Wayne?' He waited, then shook his head. 'Piece of cake.' He smiled. 'And judging from what's in here,' he patted an invisible container, 'I'd say it was a bloody big slice of cake.' His voice changed with dramatic haste. 'Oh, bloody hell, what's happened? Arnie, you all right? Arnie? Arnie?'

Lauren watched as Terry's hand went out, index finger poised, as if taking someone's pulse. 'Wayne, I think he's snuffed it. We'd better tie him up anyway and then get out of here as fast as we can.'

When the stranger was satisfied that Terry had finished speaking, he extended one hand, palm downwards. The first two fingers spread in a horizontal V formation. For a second, Lauren thought he was going to poke Terry in the eye, but instead he fixed her mother's partner with that disconcerting fixed gaze. Almost immediately, Terry sat on the sofa and resumed the docile position he had adopted before the visitor requested the one-act monologue.

'Did you get all that, Lauren? Is it clear?'

She jumped with surprise. She hadn't expected the question, and she noticed that his voice had changed. Gone was the commanding whiplash with which he addressed the men. In its place was a tender, caressing tone.

'Er … yes, I think so. He did say Towlers, didn't he?'

'That's right. Ten years ago today, these two, along with one of the security guards, robbed the store after it closed on Christmas Eve, when they knew the safe would be full. Unfortunately, the guard, Arnie Sykes,

53

had a heart attack, collapsed, and died.'

'What happened to the other man? The other guard, I mean. Did they hurt him?'

The stranger smiled, as if pleased by her concern. 'No, he wasn't hurt, not in the physical sense. But he was sentenced to fifteen years in prison, because the jury believed the prosecution claims that he was the inside man who had let the others in. His name was Butler, Danny Butler.'

'But that's not fair, if he was innocent. Why didn't these two go to jail?'

'You'll soon discover that life isn't fair, Lauren. They didn't go to prison because there was insufficient evidence to convict them, even though the police were sure they were the ones involved. Just to make sure there's no misunderstanding, let them tell you.'

He turned back and stood in front of Terry. When he spoke, his voice had returned to the whiplash command. 'Terry, tell Lauren who did the Towlers robbery ten years ago. Tell her now.'

'It was me, Lauren. Me, Wayne, and Arnie Sykes.'

'What about Danny Butler?' Lauren asked.

The stranger smiled approvingly at her.

'Nah!' Terry's tone was dismissive, as if Butler was unimportant. 'Butler had nothing to do with it. Didn't stop the judge sending him down, though. Me and Wayne pissed ourselves laughing. I still chuckle when I think of him doing a long stretch when he had no part of it.'

The visitor looked at Lauren. 'I told you they weren't very nice men.'

'You didn't need to,' Lauren replied. 'I already knew. I just didn't realise how bad.'

This time the visitor's smile was one of infinite sadness. 'Unfortunately, you haven't heard the worst of it, yet. Prepare yourself, what you're about to hear will make your blood curdle. Are you ready?'

Lauren nodded.

His attention returned to the men, who were both staring at him fixedly, their eyes never wavering. It was almost as if he was holding them captive, even though their only restraints were his voice, and those strange, pale eyes.

'OK, Wayne, it's your turn now. I want you to tell Lauren about last Christmas Eve. Let's start with the message you got. That was what kicked everything off, wasn't it?'

'It was a couple of weeks before Christmas; I was in the Red Lion. The Lion is always busy on Fridays, but it was totally packed when I walked in. There was a real shindig going on and it looked as if some of the drinkers had been there ages. Then someone told me why. Jack Wood had been released from Felling that day. He'd been serving a five for GBH. I hadn't been there long when Jack came over to talk to me.'

Wayne paused and licked his lips nervously before going on to the next bit. Instantly, the stranger extended his right arm again in that curious gesture that seemed to command total obedience.

Wayne continued. 'All right, Jack? Good to see you out and about again.'

There was silence for a second or two, then, 'How

55

do you mean, you've got a message for me? Is that what you said? It's hard to hear with all this racket going on.' Wayne looked round and raised his voice. 'Quiet, you lot, I'm trying to talk to Jack.'

His tone lowered as he said, 'Go on. You've got a message. What message? Who from?' He grinned. 'I know a few in Felling.'

Wayne listened to a voice only he could hear before continuing, 'Who said that? Butler? Who's Butler? Oh, you mean Danny Butler. How the hell did he find out about us? Anyway, thanks for the tip-off.'

Wayne stood up and made a curious gesture with his arms, which Lauren guessed was him simulating walking. He stopped, lifted his left hand, and started jabbing at the palm with the index finger of his other hand. It took Lauren a few seconds before she realized that Wayne was dialling a number on his mobile – except for the fact that he wasn't holding a phone. He raised his hand to his ear, obviously listening. After a few seconds, he spoke. 'Tel, it's Wayne. Yeah, I'm outside the Lion. I couldn't hear myself think in there, let alone talk to anyone. Listen, will you? This is important. I've just been talking to Jack Wood. Yeah, he got out this morning, that's why they're having a do for him. Anyway, that's not the point. Jack came over to give me a message. Well, it's for both of us really. It's a warning. Someone in Felling is after our blood, big style. No, no it isn't any of the drugs lot. They're all behaving themselves. The threat came from Danny Butler. Remember Butler, do you? Yes, that Danny Butler. Seems someone's blabbed to him that we were the two behind the masks when Towlers got done over. How the hell do I know who told him? But I know this, if I find the bastard I'll skin him alive.'

Wayne listened for a moment or two. 'Yes, I know there's bugger all he can do from in there, but he won't be inside for ever, will he? Fifteen, it was, but he's done eight already, and if he gets time off, he'll be back here before long.'

After another short silence, Wayne said, 'I think we should have a meet, sooner the better, and decide what we're going to do about him. OK, where and when? Yes, tomorrow.'

He lowered his hand, and began his curious arm motion again. Lauren found it odd to watch a man simulating walking while standing absolutely still. However, she had little time to dwell on this, as Wayne was already speaking. 'Hiya, Tel, what can I get you? OK.' He turned to an invisible barman. 'Two pints of Export.' He held his hand out and apparently waited for some change, before passing a non-existent pint of lager to an invisible Terry, then gesturing to the corner of a room only he could see. 'Let's sit over there in the window, that way nosy bastards can't overhear us.'

Wayne sat next to Terry, and shuffled slightly on the sofa, obviously making himself comfortable in the window of the bar. 'According to what Jack told me, Butler's sworn we'll be dead meat the minute he gets out. I asked around this morning, and folk say you don't want to mess with him. He's got an evil reputation. He was a bouncer at Macy's Club before

57

he worked at Towlers, and one or two got done over by him. I don't fancy tangling with the likes of him, so I thought we should send him a warning message. Something on the lines of, "this is what you can expect if you come near us". What do you reckon?'

Lauren was becoming accustomed to the short silences, the breaks in conversation. It was a little like hearing one end of a phone call, she thought. Her attention wandered momentarily, but returned in no uncertain manner when she took in the gist of Wayne's next remark.

'Yeah, I do have an idea. The best way to get at Butler would be through his wife and kids. If they feel threatened, they'll go running to Butler and that should stop his gallop. What's even better is they live near you on the estate, only a couple of streets away.'

Lauren gasped aloud. From the moment she had heard the name Butler it had sounded familiar. Now she knew why. She dragged her gaze from Wayne and stared at the stranger, an expression of mounting horror on her face. The incident from last year was still fresh in her memory, and the implication behind what Wayne had said was only too clear. The visitor returned her gaze, nodding in silent confirmation that her worst fears were about to be realised. He gestured to her to continue watching, and as she shifted her gaze to Wayne, he got to his feet and she saw him going through another mimed action.

He was silent now, doing something she couldn't work out for a moment. Then, as if to underline the suspicion she still hoped was wrong, she recognized what he was doing, and his words added extra confirmation – extra horror – extra revulsion. He was unscrewing the cap from a petrol can, then pouring the contents, slowly.

His voice was a mere whisper. Even from less than three yards away Lauren had to strain to catch what he was saying, all the time wishing she did not have to, but somehow the stranger's commands overrode her own abhorrence. 'OK, Tel, light that piece of paper and shove it through the letterbox. As soon as it gets going, we scarper. By the time anyone notices, we'll be safe and snug back in the Lion with plenty of witnesses to swear we hadn't moved from there all night. Go for it, Tel. Ready? Bloody Hell, that went up fast. Move it, Tel!'

Instead of returning Wayne to his catatonic state, the stranger looked at Terry. 'Just so that we've got this clear: you were with Wayne last Christmas Eve and the two of you set the fire that killed Sandra Butler and her children. Right?'

'Yeah, we did that.' Terry's voice was a dull monotone, with no inflexion or emotion whatsoever.

'And you also did the Towlers robbery?'

'Yeah, we did that as well.'

The visitor had turned to Wayne. 'You agree with that?'

'Yeah, we did 'em both.' Wayne's voice was equally toneless.

'There's something else though, isn't there? Something you've failed to mention. You agreed to tell everything, you should have realised by now that holding back will not be tolerated. So, will one of you explain about the allotment?'

Lauren thought that nothing could surprise her after what she had heard, but the mention of an allotment had her completely baffled.

'Sorry,' they mumbled.

Wayne began to explain. 'It was Tel's idea. We knew the cops would be looking for the money after we'd done the Towlers job, so we decided we'd turn some of the cash into gear. Not to use, although we did a bit. To sell, and we needed somewhere to hide the stash. We were lucky, because we got an allotment almost as soon as we put our name down. Actually, it wasn't our name at all. We used good old John Smith.

'And we put the drugs and cash in a hiding place inside the shed we've stocked up when we need to,' Terry took over the story. 'Wayne does a bit of gardening up there, grows a few veg, so he's always on hand when we have stuff to deal.'

He stopped speaking, and looked at the stranger, who stared back in silence. Although no words passed between them, Terry gave an apologetic shrug. 'OK,' he said after a couple of seconds, 'the allotment is number six. It's the last one on the left as you go in from the Barwell Gardens end.'

Having heard them out, the visitor extended both arms, one pointing at each of them, his fingers spread in that curious gesture. They fell silent, staring ahead into vacant space. He watched them for a moment, before turning to look at the girl.

'Have you heard enough?'

She gulped a deep breath to control the nausea she felt. 'More than enough,' she told him. 'I feel sick.' Her voice was little more than a croak.

'That's understandable. The point is, will you be able to remember everything they said well enough to repeat it when the time comes?'

This time her voice was clearer, her message unmistakeable. 'I don't think I shall forget a word of what was said for as long as I live, no matter how much I want to.'

The stranger smiled, a world of sadness reflected in his eyes as he told her, 'Believe me, Lauren, the memory will fade, given time. Other things will overtake it, happier things that will thrust this to the back of your mind. Now, I think it's time for you to leave.'

'Leave?' Lauren was startled by the suggestion. 'Why should I leave?'

'Oh yes, I can assure you there is no way you want to stay here. Not now, and not with what's about to happen.'

'Will they be punished for what they did?'

'Oh yes,' – the stranger smiled – 'and their punishment will last a long time. An eternity, you could say.'

He shepherded her into the hallway. When they reached the front door, he told her, 'Here's what I want you to do. Go down to the end of the street and along the main road to where the bus from the town centre stops. By the time you arrive there, your mother will be waiting to cross the road. Your job is to stop her, and make sure neither of you come near this house until later.'

'How much later?'

He smiled again. 'That will become clear.' As he spoke he opened the door and peered out. The fog was, if anything, even thicker. 'Hang on, you'll need a coat. This fog chills you through to the bone.' He took her coat from the pegs alongside the door and helped her put it on. 'Thank you for acting as my witness, Lauren. I won't see you again, but I wish you all the very best for the future. I hope you will have a long and happy life. You deserve it, for you have a good heart.'

'I still don't know your name.'

This time, the stranger's laugh was one of genuine amusement, although Lauren couldn't think of anything remotely funny in what she'd said. 'That's true, you don't,' was all he replied. He pushed her gently out of the door, guiding her towards the path. 'Oh, one final thing, will you please tell Luke I'm sorry for all the trouble I've caused him over Christmas?'

'Luke? Luke who?'

'You'll know when you meet him. Now go, or your mother will be there before you.'

Lauren walked slowly down the path, her mind whirling with everything she had witnessed in the house. She was walking slowly enough to hear the door shut, to hear the tumblers click as the stranger turned the key in the lock. She heard the muted thud as he slid the bolts home and wondered why he chose to do that. She was no nearer finding an explanation when she reached the street corner, and headed along the main road, where yet another surprise awaited her.

Quite why she should be surprised, given the astonishing things she had seen and heard over the past hour, Lauren wasn't really sure. However, exactly as the visitor had predicted, when Lauren reached the street corner and peered through the fog, there was her mother on the opposite side of the road, waiting for a lone taxi to creep past before attempting the crossing.

Lauren waved and called out. She saw her mother's surprised expression, but waited for her to cross in safety. In answer to her mother's worried enquiries, she reassured her. 'Yes, Mum, I'm fine. No, there hasn't been any trouble. At least, I don't think so. The thing is, we can't go home yet. I promised we wouldn't. The man said we shouldn't.'

Her mother stopped in her tracks. 'Man, what man? Has someone been pestering you?' She was alarmed. 'Is this man some friend of *his*?'

'No, Mum, that's not it at all.'

'Then why can't we go home?'

The way her mother referred to Terry spoke volumes for the state of their relationship. Lauren had thought recently that it might be reaching breaking point. From Lauren's point of view, that couldn't come fast enough. And that was before the events of the afternoon. Lauren rejoiced silently, then remembered the stranger's question – and her response.

'If you had the choice, what would happen to these two?'

'I wish they would disappear from out of my life and my Mum's forever.'

She shivered, an involuntary reaction, almost as if she knew what she had wished for might come true.

'Lauren, we ought to go home now. It's Christmas Eve and I've still got loads to do. I know this is probably the wrong time to say this, but I've been doing a lot of thinking, and as soon as the holiday is over, I'm going to tell him to clear out. It's my house; I've had enough of his sponging off me, and bringing his dodgy friends round. They're a bad influence, and I can't have them near you.' She slipped her arm around the girl's shoulder and held her. 'OK?' Lauren nodded her agreement. 'So, come on, let's get out of this lousy fog and into the warm.' She started to walk in the direction of the street.

'No, Mum.' Lauren caught her by the arm. 'That's fine, about Terry, I mean. But we can't go home yet. I promised the man we wouldn't.'

Her mother started at her intently. 'There you go again, talking about this mystery man who issues orders preventing me from going into my own house. Who is he? Or is he some figment of your imagination? You haven't been in the room when Terry and his friends have been smoking dodgy tobacco, have you?'

The idea that her mum thought she might be high on pot made Lauren giggle. The sound was cut short by the strident tones of a siren. Somehow, although the emergency vehicle was a long distance away, Lauren knew where it was headed; knew instinctively that it was in some way connected to her, to her house, and to the stranger who was locked in there with those two loathsome creeps.

With the wailing siren growing ever closer, Lauren persuaded her mother that they should wait. 'I don't know who the man is, but he knows everything about us. He knows all about the dreadful things Terry and Wayne did. He knew all about you having to go back to work, and how long you would be gone, and he even knew that when I got to this corner, you would be waiting to cross the road.'

It was the statement about work that convinced Lauren's mother. Convinced her, and made her shiver with fear. Lauren sensed her unease. 'What's wrong, Mum?'

'I don't know, but this is totally weird. You remember the text I got calling me back into work? I read it out to you. Well, that text described the problem quite accurately. I already had an idea what the solution would be and it was easily put right. The thing is, when I got there everyone was surprised to see me. They said they had been on the point of phoning me when I walked through the door. That was when I asked them who had sent the text. Everyone denied it, so I got my mobile out and the message had disappeared. I thought I must have deleted it, but now I'm not sure.'

'I don't think you did, Mum.' Lauren explained about the texts that Wayne and Terry had said they received, which when they checked their mobiles, had also vanished.

As mother and daughter stared at one another, perplexed and troubled by the strange occurrences, their ears were assailed by the deafening blast of a fire engine's siren. The vehicle, followed closely by a second, swept round the corner and headed up their street. Their flashing beacons and headlights were on full beam, reflecting back from the white wall of fog ahead.

They heard the sirens die away as the fire engines slowed to a halt beyond the range of their vision, making it impossible to judge where exactly the emergency was. The fog was thicker than ever, Lauren thought, and then, with a fresh thrill of fear, realized that it wasn't fog, but smoke. At that moment a whisper of breeze, no more than a zephyr, ruffled her hair. The movement of the air, slight though it was, brought the smell of smoke to her nostrils. A momentary panic came over her. What if Terry or the stranger had set fire to the house ...? She dismissed the idea as ludicrous, it was only then that she remembered the elusive aroma given off by the visitor as he passed close to her. It had been the scent of smoke.

Another thought suddenly occurred to her. She turned to her mother. 'If the problem at work was so easily solved, how come you were away so long?'

Her mother stared at her in surprise. 'What do you mean, so long? I've only been gone half an hour. I think I should have bought you a new watch for Christmas. What time do you think it is?'

Lauren hadn't actually checked her watch before.

She glanced at it now, staring in disbelief at the hands on the dial. For a moment she thought it had stopped. Then she saw the second hand moving regularly round the dial. No, it hadn't stopped, and her mother was quite right. It had only been half an hour or so since her mother had left the house. But everything that had happened couldn't have taken place in so short a time, surely? That was impossible.

Slowly, reluctantly, mother and daughter began to walk down the street, towards where the engines had come to rest. They had only gone a few paces when another siren warned them of the approach of another emergency vehicle. Almost as soon as they heard it, a gaudily painted estate car, lights flashing, hurtled past. Its brake lights came on, and as it slowed, they had time to read the sign on the back. 'Ambulance responder,' Lauren's mother said, 'that's bad news for someone. I hope we're not going to have a repetition of last year's tragedy.'

Her sentiments were being echoed inside the vehicle. 'I can't believe we're having a call out to another Christmas Eve fire so close to where the other one was,' the paramedic who was driving told his passenger. 'Makes you wonder if it's the same sick bastard. I know what I'd do with him if I caught him.'

Paula Morton remembered the story. 'That was the mother and two children, wasn't it? I heard about it at the planning meeting. Was that fire around here as well?'

'A couple of streets away, Doc. I don't think anyone involved in the operation had a happy

Christmas last year. Perils of the job, I suppose.'

They were slowing to a halt when Morton noticed the woman and girl walking alongside them. She wondered briefly if they might be neighbours, or even worse, if it was their house she and her colleague had been called to.

Lauren and her mother followed in the wake of the car, their thoughts beginning to darken as they passed house after house. The fog lifted briefly, and Lauren's mother glimpsed the vague shadows of the firemen. 'Lauren! It's our house. Look!'

As the fog lifted a little more, the horrified pair saw firemen busy unreeling and deploying the hoses, while closer at hand, a police officer was setting up an exclusion zone using incident tape. He stepped into their path to prevent them getting any closer.

'That's our house!' Lauren's mother told him, her voice reflecting the panic both she and Lauren felt.

'Hang on.' He turned and shouted to one of the firemen. 'Jim, householder is here.'

The man who had been directing operations hurried over. 'Is anyone inside the building?' he asked.

Prompted by her mother, Lauren responded. 'There are three men in there.'

'Are they all mobile?'

Lauren was confused, thinking of phones, then she understood. 'Yes, yes, they can all move about OK, although two of them could be drunk.'

'What about entrances? Are they all clear?'

'The front door is locked and bolted,' Lauren added. 'I heard the man lock and bolt it as I was leaving to meet my mum.'

'And the back door won't open,' Lauren's mother told him. 'The wood's warped and swollen from all the damp weather.'

'It'll open for us,' he replied grimly. 'Right, thanks.' The fireman swung round and moved smartly away, issuing a volley of commands to two men already dressed in breathing apparatus. 'You two, round the back. Take sledges and axes, you'll need to break the door down.' Almost as an afterthought, he looked back and asked Lauren, 'Where were they? Whereabouts in the house?'

'In the lounge. At least, that was where two of them were. The other one, he was in the hallway.'

He pressed the button on his radio. 'Concentrate on the lounge. Try and reach that if you can.'

He hurried back to supervise the men who were nearly ready to begin playing jets of water onto the flames they could see through the window. They heard the sound of breaking glass and splintering wood as the back door was being assaulted.

Moments later the chief's radio crackled into life. 'Chief, Chief, hang on. There is no fire!'

'What do you mean? No fire? We can see the flames from here.' He turned and looked back at the window – but the flames were gone. 'What the hell is going on in there,' he demanded.

'I'm telling you, there's no fire in this house.' He continued with the grim message, 'But we've found the two men in the lounge. We're going to need the doc and paramedic in here. I think these two are goners. No sign of a third man. Tom's checking the other rooms.'

The chief signalled to two people standing by the responder vehicle who immediately approached him. One was dressed in the distinctive uniform of a paramedic. The other, a woman in an orange boiler suit and hi-vis jacket with 'Doctor' emblazoned across the back was carrying a small holdall.

Lauren and her mother continued to watch and listen, as a new voice joined in, his words muffled slightly by the breathing apparatus he was wearing. 'Tom here, I've checked everywhere, there's definitely no fire inside the building and I can't find the third man. No way he could have got out of the back, and the front door's locked and bolted. Are you sure the kid wasn't mistaken?'

Lauren was adamant, even when the fire officer suggested her imagination was running riot. He had little time to press his questions, assuming the man had left before they arrived. He set off with the medical team for the interior of the house, to determine exactly what had happened.

The firemen now without their breathing apparatus were standing in the kitchen. 'Look, I've no idea what's going on, any more than you. You can still smell the smoke,' the first man said.

'I know that, I'm not stupid. But where's the seat of the fire? Even if it had burnt itself out, there would still be scorching. Besides, there were far too many flames for that.'

The chief intervened. 'There must be an

explanation and our investigators will sort it out but in the meantime you can sweep up the mess you've made round that door.'

The men shuffled off, still debating the lack of logic to anything they had witnessed.

A third fireman entered the kitchen. 'Doctor's had a look at the two in the lounge. Both dead, I'm afraid. She wants to see you immediately.'

In the lounge, Paula Morton told the chief, 'These men did not die from any fire. Smell the air; you'll barely get a whiff of smoke. So if fire didn't kill them, something else did. I think we should categorize these as suspicious deaths, report this as a crime scene, and call the police in. The post-mortem will confirm cause of death, but I can guarantee it wasn't fire or smoke inhalation.'

She noticed the slight hesitation. 'I'll need to inform the pathologist anyway. I'll make the calls, shall I?'

Her first call was to Dr Austin, the pathologist. He was less than happy about having to turn out on Christmas Eve. Paula, who had been warned about him, knew this was largely for show. Having persuaded Austin to attend, she searched her contacts for Luke Sharp's number and dialled it.

'Luke, it's Paula Morton. No, sorry, this is business. I'm at Castleton Street on the Normanton estate. House number is forty-seven. I think you should come out here. There's been a supposed house fire – I'll let the Fire Officer explain that one – but the two men who died weren't victims of a fire. No, I don't know the cause of death. It could be natural, but I doubt it. OK, see you soon.'

When Luke Sharp arrived in Castleton Street one of the fire engines was leaving the scene. Paula Morton was standing close to the second engine, deep in conversation with a woman and teenage girl. Firemen were packing away their unused equipment.

He parked up and walked over to greet the doctor. 'Dr Morton, what's all this about a supposed fire?'

'Speak to the CFO, he'll explain.' She then introduced her companions. 'This lady is the tenant of the house, and also partner of one of the deceased.'

Sharp noted that the woman showed little sign of distress at her recent bereavement, but listened as Paula continued, 'She was out when the incident happened. However, her daughter Lauren was in the house until shortly before the fire was reported.'

She turned to the mother and daughter. 'I'll leave you with Detective Sergeant Sharp. He'll need to ask you some questions, but don't worry, he's very nice.'

'Before I do anything else I ought to take a look inside,' Sharp said.

'There is one thing you should be aware of: there are two bodies inside. However, Lauren is adamant that when she left, there was a third man there, someone she'd never seen before. There is some confusion here, as the fire officers cannot work out how he got out of the building.' She didn't add 'if he was ever in there'; but left Sharp to work that out for himself. 'Dr Austin is inside, and he's not very happy.'

'According to my colleagues he never is.'

'Doc, we're needed,' the paramedic called out.

'I've got to go,' Paula said, and turned to leave. 'However, I do want a word with you when I'm free.'

'Thank you, Dr Morton. Just let me know when.' He turned to Lauren and her mother. 'We can't leave you standing here, hang on a minute.' He turned and waved to a constable who had been controlling traffic, what little there was in a side street. 'Is that your car?' he pointed down the street.

'Yes, sir.'

'In that case, please take these two ladies and sit them inside it out of the cold.'

Lauren smiled at the thought she was a 'lady'.

Sharp continued, 'I'll be as quick as I can. Then we ought to see about finding you some accommodation.'

He noted their look of surprise, and explained, 'For the time being our forensic officers and those from the fire service will need to examine the property and determine exactly what's happened.'

He turned to go towards the house, where one of the firemen directed him to the rear of the building. 'The front door's locked and bolted like we found it. The chief wants it kept that way. Be careful going through the back door. We had to break it down to get in. Watch out for splinters and broken glass.'

In the lounge, Austin was inspecting the corpses before they were moved into body bags for transport to the mortuary. He greeted Sharp with a grunt that might have been 'hello', but certainly wasn't 'Merry Christmas'.

Sharp looked over Austin's shoulder at one of the bodies. Although he was used to the results of sudden and violent death, he recoiled in shock. He had never seen an expression such as the one on the victim's face. It was a look of pure terror. He glanced to his left, towards the other corpse, and was astonished to see a similar expression on the face of the second victim. What, he wondered, could have caused such fear, or was it some strange by-product of the way they'd died?

'Any idea as to cause of death? Dr Morton isn't satisfied that it's due to fire,' Sharp asked Austin.

'What fire? You'll have to wait for the post-mortem.'

'When will that be?'

'Tomorrow.'

'What time?'

'No idea, I won't be doing it. The only body I intend to carve tomorrow will be the turkey my wife will attempt to cremate. There's a roster of Home Office pathologists and the one on duty will carry out the post-mortem. When I take these two back to the mortuary I'll contact the right person and get them to call you with a time.'

Sharp turned to the chief fire officer, who seemed keen to talk to him. 'This is a really weird going-on,' the fireman said. 'The girl who lives here swears there was a third man in the house, and that he let her out and locked up after she'd gone, but we can find no trace of him or how he got out. The front door is bolted, the back door was impassable, and all the windows are locked.'

'Maybe one of the dead men let him out after she left?'

The fireman stared at him. 'Good Lord, I never thought of that. Do you think the girl might be responsible for any of this?'

'No idea. Anything else I should know?'

The chief hesitated. 'When we arrived we could see the flames through the window here in this room and were sure the whole house was about to go up. I sent in two men to try and find the occupants before we turned the jets on, but when they got in this room there was no fire. They said there was a trace of smoke in here, but certainly not enough to cause those deaths. Added to which I've never seen fire victims look like those two,' – he shivered – 'and I hope I never do again. I've ordered an investigation team to check for the source of a fire, but whatever killed those two poor souls in there, I'm prepared to bet it wasn't fire.'

'Is this some sort of elaborate hoax, do you think?'

'Has to be, I can't see any other reason. There's no damage to the property, by the way, which is another oddity. I can't work out how such an apparently intense blaze, that we all saw through the window, might I add, didn't flash through the house.'

'I've also ordered a SOCO team here. Let's hope between them, your scientists and ours come up with some answers. I'm off now. I want to get the tenant and her daughter out of the way before Austin's men bring the bodies out.'

He headed back to the police car and told the

officer he would drive Lauren and her mother to the station. As he ushered them to his car he turned to Lauren's mother. 'We'll make you a cup of tea, or whatever you want, then arrange somewhere for you to stay.'

Back at the station Sharp asked the duty sergeant to contact social services and the council to search for temporary accommodation. 'I suspect there'll only be the duty officer available but do your best. If we can't find anywhere else, we're a bit stuck,' he commented, 'unless you've room down there.' He pointed to the corridor leading to the cells.

'You're joking, aren't you? I was already thinking of hanging a "no vacancies" sign on the front door.'

At that moment the strains of a Christmas carol could be heard filtering along the corridor; the drunken rendition, completely out of tune.

'Office worker,' the sergeant said. 'Finished work early,' he added by way of explanation.

'I wonder if he knows "Silent Night"?' Luke said as he walked away.

Sharp took Lauren and her mother to his office. 'It's more comfortable than downstairs, and you won't be disturbed here.' He got them both a cup of tea, apologising for the quality the vending machine produced. They hadn't finished their drinks when the sergeant rang through. 'I've got them accommodation. The Blacksmith's Arms has a twin room; the council were useless so I used my initiative.'

'Right, that's great. I'll take them there.' He turned to Lauren's mother. 'You've had a nasty shock so I'll get someone to take your statements later.'

Having seen them safely installed, Sharp returned to his office and picked up the phone. 'I need a female officer to pop round to the Castleton Street house with the tenant. She and her daughter need a change of clothing and there's something to do with hidden presents. Yes, apparently it's nearly Christmas,' Luke laughed as he replaced the handset, muttering 'Bah humbug' under his breath.

About half an hour later, Paula Morton arrived. She accepted the coffee Sharp offered her, and as she sipped it, told him what had been said as she waited outside the house for him to arrive. 'Lauren told me about the man in the house. She said he seemed to have a hold over the others, as if he'd hypnotised them.'

'Could that account for the look on their faces, perhaps?' Luke shivered. 'That was scary.'

'I couldn't say. I've seen plenty of dead people before, but never looking like that. Perhaps this mystery man did hypnotise them. According to Lauren he made them confess to all sorts of things, and wanted Lauren as a witness.'

'That sounds weird. Did she say what they confessed to?'

Paula told him the details and Luke started at her in disbelief. Then she added, 'If you think that's weird, wait for the next bit. Lauren was upset, thinking that nobody would believe her. So I said "you'll be fine. Just tell the truth".'

'That's fair enough, nothing weird about it. Except

this whole thing is weird.'

'Hang on, I haven't finished. Lauren said as she was leaving the house, "the strange man told me to give his apologies to Luke for all the trouble he was causing over Christmas". Those were her exact words. I know for a fact she hadn't heard your Christian name before.'

'That really is weird. Perhaps Lauren's story isn't imagination after all.'

'What will you do about it?'

'I'm going to pull those case files and read them. It might give a clue as to who this mystery man is, if he exists. It'll pass the time until the PM.'

Sharp spent Christmas morning reading the files, and at around the time most people were beginning their Christmas dinner, he arrived at the mortuary, where the duty pathologist, a cheerful Scot who seemed glad to be away from the bosom of his family, carried out the twin procedures. He reported his findings to Sharp in the grim little office alongside the examination room. Sharp listened to him in disbelief. 'Are you absolutely certain?' he asked.

The pathologist looked at Sharp for a moment, and smiled. 'I am absolutely certain. Unless the toxicology proves different, both those men are completely healthy. I strongly suspect we may find traces of alcohol and possibly some recreational use of narcotics but there is no physical reason for their deaths.'

'I saw the expression on their faces, as if they were frightened. Could they have had heart attacks?'

'No, there's no evidence of that. But there is one odd thing. Mentioning their faces reminded me.' He led Sharp back into the examination room and pointed to the corpses. 'Rigor mortis has worn off now. Normally when that happens, the facial muscles relax, giving the dead person a calm, peaceful look. As you can see, that hasn't happened here. Don't ask me to explain why, but it's almost as if the terror they felt is still affecting them.'

Sharp needed answers. He called the station from the mortuary and asked the duty officer to contact the Blacksmith's Arms. 'I need to speak to the girl and her mother ASAP. Ask them to come to the station will you?'

When he returned from the mortuary, Sharp found Lauren waiting, along with her mother, ready to give her statement. He summoned a female police officer to attend the interview, and invited Lauren to tell her story. Eventually, he asked her for a description of the stranger.

Her reply was detailed enough to send Sharp scurrying back to his office. He returned to the interview room a few minutes later and nodded to the officer, who restarted the tape. 'Is this the man you saw at the house, Lauren?' Sharp asked, placing a photograph on the table.

Lauren identified the man immediately. 'There's something else,' she added. 'I almost forgot about the allotment.'

Sharp looked puzzled. 'What allotment?'

'The one where they keep the drugs. Wayne told

the man it was number six, the last one on the left as you go in from Barwell Gardens.'

'That could be very useful, thank you.'

Sharp ended the interview there. He had only been back in his office a few minutes when he received a further shock, via a phone call from the fire service. 'It's about that allotment shed fire last night.'

Sharp didn't speak, his mind was whirling. 'What shed fire?'

'Sorry, I thought you knew. Didn't your lot tell you about the fingerprints? They match both victims of the Castleton Street blaze.'

Sharp remained silent so the officer continued. 'The blaze was similar to the house fire – except this time there really was a fire – but the damage was superficial. However, my men found a huge quantity of what we believe to be Class A drugs hidden inside, which we've passed to your people for testing.'

Sharp was still coming to terms with this news when he received an email from the SOCO team, informing him the only fingerprints from within the house were those of Lauren, her mother, and the two victims. This cast doubt on Lauren's story. By now, Sharp didn't know what to believe.

On Boxing Day, the fire chief called him. 'Our forensic guys could find no trace of a fire at the house. As of this moment, there is no apparent cause for what we saw.'

'Is there any chance it was reflected light you saw? Maybe the Christmas tree lights?'

'We *all* saw flames, and no, it wasn't festive lights

of any sort. Besides which, the tree wasn't even plugged in. And before you ask, we had not been partaking of the Christmas spirit! And here's another thing for you to puzzle over.'

'What more can there be?'

'Just before we left the scene, a bloke in a handyman's van turned up.'

'And?'

'He'd come to fix the back door.'

'I don't see the problem with that, the house would need to be secure. Who sent for him?'

'Nobody. Well nobody that should have, that is.'

'You'd better explain.'

'He said a bloke phoned and booked the callout first thing that morning. He'd confirmed by text message. When I said I didn't believe him he showed me the text – except there wasn't one!'

'This just gets stranger by the minute.'

'If you think that, wait until you hear the rest. As a matter of course, I got one of my chaps to check the treble nine call in the hope of finding who made it. Unfortunately, there's no trace of it.'

'How do you mean?'

'I mean that the phone call that sent our engines to Castleton Street simply doesn't exist. I got the emergency operator to check the recording, and all they could hear was some sort of static hiss. The only thing we have is the operator remembers it was a man's voice. Don't ask me to explain, because I can't, so if you can come up with anything, I'd love to hear it.'

Sharp was thoroughly confused. Every new piece of evidence either added strength to Lauren's story or undermined it. Acting on impulse, he made a phone call, the result of which left his mind reeling.

Two days after Boxing Day, having received further information from the pathologist, Luke typed up his report and took it to Detective Superintendent Parker. 'I don't know what you'll make of it, Geoff, because I can't find a logical explanation for any of it.'

Back at his desk, he phoned Paula Morton's mobile. 'Any chance you could meet me for a drink this evening?'

She agreed, and at seven on the dot, arrived at the Three Tuns. Sharp was already there, looking tired and bewildered, she thought. 'How's the investigation going?' she asked.

'It isn't going. It's stalled. In fact, it's damned near in reverse. I'm completely baffled by the whole business.' Sharp outlined the facts he had gathered, ticking them off on his fingers as he spoke. 'There is no identifiable cause for the fire everyone claims to have witnessed, no trace of an accelerant, faulty wiring, cigarette ends, candles left burning, anything.

'Neither is there any apparent cause for the death of the victims. I did wonder if they might have been poisoned, but the results were negative for any form of toxin. The post-mortem also ruled out fire as the cause, or the effects of smoke inhalation. My only clue is that expression on the victims' faces. If I had to speculate, I'd suggest they died of fright, but I suppose that wouldn't hold water with you medical people.'

'I don't think you're likely to see it on a death certificate,' Paula agreed. 'Is there anything else odd?'

'The whole thing is odd.' Luke shook his head, then took a gulp at his pint before he continued. 'Added to what I've already told you, there is no trace of Lauren's mystery man ever having entered the property. The only prints in the house are those we expected to find. There was also an allotment fire on Christmas Eve in the very place Lauren told me they had confessed was where they kept drugs. This time there really was a fire but they can't determine the cause and there was very little damage. However, they did find a huge cache of drugs and the dead men's prints in the shed.'

Sharp paused and took another gulp of his beer. 'Now we come to the weirdest bit of all. When I interviewed Lauren, I showed her a photograph of a man matching her description of the mysterious stranger. She made a positive identification of him immediately.'

'Who was it?'

'Danny Butler, the security guard imprisoned for the robbery, whose wife and kids were killed in that house fire a year ago. Her description was correct, right down to the last detail, and Butler was not the sort you could easily confuse with anyone else.' Sharp went on to describe Butler's appearance.

'I see what you mean. Then there can't be any chance that Lauren got the wrong man. That makes it easy enough for you, though. All you have to do is find him and ask him to explain how the two men died in such suspicious circumstances.'

Sharp shook his head. 'That's what I thought, so I rang Felling Prison to ask when Butler was released. It turns out that, Danny Butler still had several months of his sentence to go.'

'So he couldn't have been the man Lauren saw, if he's still in prison.'

'He was – and he wasn't,' Sharp told her.

'How do you mean? He was either in prison or out, surely?'

'Technically, I suppose you could say he'd been released, if released is the correct word. Danny Butler died of a heart attack the day before Christmas Eve.'

The Proof of the Pudding

Jane Wenham-Jones

'I don't think I'll bother with a pudding this year,' I said – more to myself than anyone else. I looked at the sticky packet of half-finished raisins I'd found lurking at the back of the larder behind the rusting treacle tin. 'It's not as if anyone eats it.'

Charlotte looked up at me in horror. 'Yes we do!' she said indignantly. Ben appeared equally startled. 'Oh, Mum!' he said disapprovingly.

'You don't!' I said. 'The birds do. And we don't really need a cake either! Look!' I added, pulling the battered old cake tin down from the shelf. 'It's October!' I yanked off the lid to reveal a remaining dark brown marzipan-topped lump. 'We've still got some left.'

'Mmmn,' said Dave, wandering into the kitchen. 'I'll have that, love. If nobody else wants it that is,' he added, already lifting it onto a plate.

'Marvellous,' he said, licking his lips ten minutes later. 'Plenty of brandy – that's the secret. Keeps for ever!'

'Mum says we can't have one this year,' said Charlotte petulantly. Dave looked at me wounded.

'It won't be Christmas without the cake,' said Charlotte dramatically, never one to miss the chance to act deprived. 'And I love making the pudding,' she finished sadly.

'What?' I spluttered. 'When was the last time you had anything to do with it? I make them both myself. On my own.'

It hadn't always been like that. Once it was a bit of a ritual in the family. We'd make the pudding and cake together. I had a sudden image of a tiny Charlotte standing on a chair so she could reach the bowl, frowning in concentration as she used both hands to wield the wooden spoon through the stiff, fruit-laden mixture. Of Ben standing quietly by the side of the table, unnoticed, stuffing his mouth with sultanas till Dave had leapt laughing towards him, swung the dish out of reach, and caught him as he staggered. 'Goodness, he'll sleep well – I've already soaked them in brandy!'

We always did it together. Waited until some grey, cold autumn afternoon when I would get out the big brown bowl that had been my grandmother's, line up the ingredients on the kitchen table, pull my favourite old recipe book down off the shelf, and check for quantities. Dave always did the measuring while I mixed. He'd line the cake tin with greaseproof paper and butter the pudding basin, the kids would pick at the dry fruit and run their fingers round the rim of the bowl, collecting the sweet, sticky leftovers. And all of them would have a turn stirring with the wooden spoon.

'Make a wish,' I would urge my children. 'But don't tell me or it won't come true!' I'd add, as I could see Charlotte's just waiting to burst from her small lips. I always knew what they'd be wishing for anyway – some Spider-man toy or impossibly-waisted Barbie doll (before they discovered iPhones and netbooks), while I'd find myself silently making some sentimental plea for their happiness or world peace, strangely moved by the raptness of their solemn faces.

I never did know what Dave wished for but he always gave me a huge wink as I placed the baking tin reverently in the oven.

And then there'd be that heavenly warmth of sugar and spice that would hang comfortingly in the air for hours while the soft, golden concoction, thick with fruit and nuts, firmed and darkened, and the pudding steamed on the hob to the gentle slurp of bubbling water.

But somehow we'd got out of the habit. Now the kids would be upstairs or out with their friends. Dave in the garden or in front of the TV. Those days had gone. Surely it would be easier just to buy a small pudding, forget about a cake …

'Well I'll help you this time then,' said Charlotte impatiently. I glanced at her in surprise. She rolled her eyes. 'I suppose.'

And there must have been something in me too that still hankered after it all. The next morning I found myself writing 'Cherries, ground almonds, brown sugar' on the shopping list even though I knew very well that come Christmas Day, everyone would have eaten too much turkey to contemplate much pudding and the cake would just sit there on the side table sporting the same plastic tree and reindeer I stuck in every year.

Dave's mum would eventually say, 'Oh, go on then, I'll just have a sliver.' Dave would rub his stomach and say, 'Sorry, love, I just couldn't eat another thing,' and neither of the children would touch a slice. And the cake would be lowered into the tin which was where it would stay for the rest of the year.

But come Sunday afternoon when it was raining, I looked out at the darkening sky and reached for the old, fat book on the shelf. Ben and Dave looked positively alarmed as I hauled them away from the football on TV, Charlotte disgusted.

'I was just going to phone Clare,' she said crossly.

'Well you can do that later,' I replied sweetly. 'Wash your hands, tie your hair back, and put that apron on – you're chief mixer!'

I saw Ben and Dave exchange dubious glances as I shoved a packet of glacé cherries and four eggs into their hands.

'Chop one, beat the other,' I instructed brightly. 'And someone start greasing the tin.'

'My arm's aching,' grumbled Charlotte as she blended sugar and butter, 'Oi! Get out of it, you loser!' she protested as her brother ducked under her arm later and fished out a fingerful of fruit-laden goo. 'Tell him to leave me alone, Mum!'

But her voice was unusually good-natured and I smiled at Dave as they shoved each other.

'Remember that Christmas when Granddad nearly swallowed the sixpence?' she asked suddenly, as I folded small squares of foil round old silver coins and we all took turns to stir and wish. Ben laughed. 'What about Dad on my skateboard after lunch? After he'd said he could show me a thing or two.' He grinned at his father. 'Showed me how to fall off more like!'

Dave punched him playfully on the shoulder as Ben stirred. 'It was that uneven pavement. Roller-skating champion, I was at school.'

'Yeah, right.' Charlotte giggled and rolled her eyes heavenwards as she took the spoon. We all fell quiet as she held her eyes shut for some moments. I could no longer be sure what she was hoping for – something more complicated these days no doubt than the latest gadget – but as I stood, waiting to fasten the cloth over the pudding basin, I looked at the dark lashes feathering her cheek and felt a strange tug of emotion.

Dave winked at me as he took over from her. 'Now what are those lottery numbers?'

'It won't come true if you tell anyone,' retorted Charlotte.

Dave handed me the spoon, giving my arm a squeeze as he did so. 'That's OK,' he said, removing a little cake mixture from Charlotte's shoulder. 'I've got all the riches I need.'

I closed my eyes and pushed the wooden handle in circles and wished for it always to stay that way …

On Christmas Day I looked at the cake marzipanned by Charlotte and rather unevenly iced by Ben, at the old plastic reindeer sitting lopsidedly in the middle, and I smiled.

Then I lifted the pudding from the steamer, placed the sprig of holly in the centre, and carefully tipped the brandy around the outside. 'Ta daa!' I cried as I placed the dish on the table, watching as the blue-tinged flames flickered around the perfect moist dome. A ring of faces looked at it.

'Oh well maybe just a tiny spoonful,' said Dave's

mum.

Dave rubbed his stomach. 'Don't think I could right now, love.'

Ben wrinkled his nose. 'Are there any roast potatoes left, Mum?' he asked hopefully. Charlotte, her mouth full of chocolate, smiled at me with bulging cheeks and silently shook her head.

Dave met my eyes.

'OK just a small bit then,' he said, pulling the cream towards him. I think he thought I'd be disappointed if he didn't. But I looked around the table at my healthy, happy children, remembered them laughing together in the kitchen, saw the warmth in Dave's eyes, and I knew I didn't care if the birds ate it all this year too.

For sometimes, the proof of the pudding isn't in the eating at all.

What the Dickens!

A Euphemia Martins Christmas Story

Caroline Dunford

NOTE TO READERS

This Christmas story takes place after *A Death for King and Country* (Euphemia Martins Mysteries Book 7), but can be read out of order without fear of spoilers!

Frost as pretty as lace outlined the edges of my window. My breath hung before me in little clouds and my fire crackled as I sat up in bed and drank my morning tea. I wondered if snow would come today. I imagined the Muller estate would look spectacular covered in white. The trees down by the lake would be particularly pretty. It seemed as if Christmas 1912 might be the best we had had for years.

The maids had been and gone about their early morning tasks and currently all was quiet. Richenda and Hans' adopted daughter, Amelia, who had been found under the most extraordinary circumstances, had finally settled into her new home thanks to the help of her temporary nursemaid, my old friend Merry. We were no longer kept awake by her cries and shouting.

All of us quite understood that the tot had been through more than most two-year-olds, but when your sleep is broken every night for several months one becomes irritable and tired. Richenda's former insistence at staying by the side of her new daughter had wrought havoc in the marital department of the Mullers' marriage to the extent the poor man had had to beg me for help in veiled, but embarrassing, terms. But all this was behind us.

My most recent adventures had concluded satisfactorily – which I confess is unusual – and I was looking forward to the prospect of a happy Christmas, safe in my position of companion to the lady of the house. Frankly, the Mullers, for various reasons, were more than generous to me, and Merry seemed to have quite forgiven me for my rise in status. We had begun as maids at the infamous Stapleford Hall, Richenda's birthplace. Merry had always been supportive of my various promotions, but now I had risen to a level that was closer to lady than servant. To complete matters Bertram, Richenda's half-brother and my unwilling, but loyal, companion in various adventures, was due to arrive to spend Christmas with us all.

Of course I would have liked to have been back home with Little Joe and Mother, but I had been able to send them a substantial amount of money, so I was assured they would be having a very merry Christmas too.

All in all, everything was right in the world. I found myself humming a carol under my breath as I used the wash-stand. Despite the fire it was cool in my room and I promised myself I would have a bath before dinner. This morning, after breakfast, Richenda, Merry, Amelia, and I were to decorate the huge tree the new head gardener had set up in the hall. Hans had spared no expense for his daughter's first Christmas here and had sent for the most expensive of tree trimmings from Harrods store. Boxes of them were downstairs waiting to be opened.

I chose my older green dress to wear. I expected that tree-trimming, especially with a toddler, might get quite messy.[1] Richenda was already at breakfast, picking at a smoked haddock on her plate, and looking glum. My heart sank.

---

[1] I do not understand how small children are always sticky. Even when there appears to be no sticky substance in sight that they could have smeared themselves with.

'Is something wrong?' I asked.

Richenda gave me a tired smile. 'I'm feeling a little under the weather this morning. It must have been something at dinner last night.'

Yes, too much cake, I thought. Richenda was extremely fond of cake. She could also be temperamental, so we were all inclined to ply her with yet more cake when she was low or difficult. I could see from her waistline that this was something all of us would have to curb. Since she had married Hans, though, and since the arrival of Amelia in particular, Richenda was improved beyond measure from the old days at Stapleford Hall, when she had been under the sway of her manipulative and, quite frankly, black-hearted brother. In contrast, she had shown herself to have a heart of gold.

'Shall we put off dressing the tree till tomorrow?' I suggested. 'It is only the eighteenth of December and many families do not decorate their tree until Christmas Eve.'

'No, I don't want to do that. Amy has been so excited about the boxes in the hall. It would be a great shame to disappoint her. I will be fine.' She pushed away the plate of haddock. 'I usually love it,' she said, 'but the smell is making me feel sick.'

'Shall I ring for some more hot toast? That always settles my stomach.' I lifted the lid of the teapot. 'And more tea. This is rather stewed.'

Richenda nodded. 'Hans came down very early this morning. There's some surprise he is arranging. He thinks I don't know anything about it.' She gave a very feminine smile. 'He can be so sweet.'

Pleased as I was for Richenda, I did not want to listen to romantic anecdotes over my breakfast. Instead I asked her about the toys ordered for Amelia. Her face softened and she began an alarmingly long list. Really, if they gave all these toys to the tot she would disappear under the mountain they made and never be seen again. However, I kept my thoughts to myself. Instead, when I could take no more about how Professor So-and-so thought it good for children to be introduced to musical instruments early in their life – a decision I knew we would all come to regret – I turned her thoughts to the estate ball for the servants and we passed the time quite happily thinking of games and treats for the staff. Richenda wanted to organise a game of blind man's buff. At that moment Stone, the appropriately named butler, came into the room and Richenda and I almost fell off our seats laughing. The idea of such a correct and serious individual playing silly Christmas games was irresistible.

Fortunately Stone had not heard our conversation and stood there stoically regarding the opposite wall until we composed ourselves. When Richenda had wiped the last tear of mirth away, Stone announced, 'Mr Bertram Stapleford is here.'

'Gosh,' said Richenda. 'I wasn't expecting him until just before dinner.'

'I cannot explain the gentleman's early arrival, ma'am, but I feel I should inform you that Mr Stapleford does not appear happy.'

'Oh,' said Richenda, somewhat taken aback. It was

most unlike Stone to venture an opinion on a guest and on a member of the family it was unheard of.

'I did not like to mention it, ma'am,' continued Stone, 'but I felt you should be warned.'

The words were barely out of his mouth before Bertram erupted into the room. His face was black as thunder and contorted in a ghastly frown. His unfortunate beard, one no one could convince him to get rid of, seemed longer in a tufty sort of way.[2]

'Damn, this bloody season!' he cried and threw himself down into a chair. 'Eggs, Stone. I want eggs. Fresh and scrambled. Toast, and coffee as black as ink.'

'At once, sir,' said Stone and left.

'It's lovely to see you too, brother,' said Richenda.

'Gah,' said Bertram.

'I beg your pardon,' said Richenda, a note of warning in her voice.

'It is fortunate you have arrived early,' I interjected, hoping to avoid a sibling spat, 'we are shortly to dress the tree with Amelia. It should be most entertaining.'

'Pah,' said Bertram, showing a little diversity in his speech, 'McLeod would be more use. He's taller.' This was said with all the bitterness of a shorter gentleman. Rory McLeod, now butler at Bertram's estate, White Orchards, and once my fiancée, was tall, broad, golden haired, and handsome. Bertram was short and dark, his

---

[2]The beard's biggest drawback was that it would not grow evenly.

delicate features taken from his French *Mama*.[3] Both men had once been rivals for my affection. Rory from real affection and Bertram out of a misplaced sense of duty. It was all terribly awkward.

'Amelia will be down shortly. She will be delighted to see you,' I said desperately. Bertram, although approving of children in general and Amelia's adoption in particular, had the natural wariness of the male towards small, unpredictable creatures.

'Hmm,' said Bertram, toning his grumpiness down slightly.

Bertram's eggs, Merry, and the aforementioned small creature arrived at the same time. Amelia ran to her mother.

'You're looking very pleased with yourself,' said Richenda. 'What have you and Merry been up to?''

''Umptious,' said Amelia.

'Christmas porridge,' explained Merry. 'She means it's scrumptious.'

'My, that's a big word,' said Bertram, trying to be avuncular. 'Scrumptious.' Amelia happily turned her attention towards him and trotted over. Bertram's eyes rolled in his head, displaying far too much white, rather like a frightened horse.

'I ate lots 'n' lots 'n' lots,' said Amelia proudly. She then gave a little hiccough. Merry and I moved as one, but we were too late. Amelia deposited a substantial portion of her breakfast in Bertram's lap.

---

[3]Though there had been nothing delicate about the nature of the lady in question, who had ruled the children with alternate disinterest and a rod of iron.

Bertram leapt to his feet, uttering a small cry of distress.

'Shall I get Stone to show you to your room?' said Richenda with all the nonchalance of a mother used to the activities of toddlers.

Bertram stood, Amelia's vomit dripping slowly down onto his shoes, and nodded forlornly.

Merry and Richenda fussed over the child, who having now lost her the contents of her stomach was asking for more porridge. I found the view out of the window most attractive. Stone whisked Bertram away without further embarrassment.

'Well, I suppose if Uncle Bertram doesn't want his eggs,' Richenda said to her daughter.

'I think perhaps a little toast, ma'am,' said Merry quickly. 'We don't want Amelia's tummy being yucky on the Christmas tree, do we?'

Amelia, having argued for jam, sat down to the task of making herself seriously sticky.

'I don't think that improved Bertram's mood,' I commented.

'No,' agreed Richenda, 'but it was rather funny.'

'I'd be surprised if you saw him before dinner,' said Merry, who having served the Staplefords since her childhood, knew Bertram's sulks of old.

Richenda poured Merry a cup of tea. When no one else was around the distinction of rank was not as defined as it should be. My mother would be horrified, but then the three of us had been through so many adventures separately and collectively that if sometimes felt as if the rules of the normal world didn't apply to us. 'I'm thinking,' said Richenda eyeing Merry meaningfully, 'that it is going to put a bit of a dampener on Christmas if Bertram continues in this frame of mind.'

'You mean we need a plan,' said Merry, grinning mischievously.

I regarded them with foreboding. 'Perhaps there is something amiss that is causing his distress,' I said.

'Other than Rory being taller?' said Richenda.

'Other than Amelia being sick?' said Merry.

'Beard bad,' said Amelia through her toast.

'Why does he persist in trying to grow it?' asked Richenda.

I shrugged. 'I have no idea.'

'Will you be wearing the lovely evening gown I had made to go with the hats I gave you last Christmas?' asked Richenda suddenly. She turned to Merry. 'I am trying to make Euphemia understand that she needs signature colours. I have chosen purple and green for her.'

'Lovely,' said Merry, her eyes sparkling, 'I'd give a lot to see that. How about a fashion show, Euphemia?'

Richenda's pet project of clothing me had on more than one occasion led to my doing an excellent impression of a mouldy cabbage. An experience I was not keen to repeat. 'So what are we going to do about Bertram?' I said, heartlessly sacrificing him in my own interest.

By the time the tree was finished we had a plan. I felt it was both highly imaginative and doomed to failure from the start. Fortunately, I would not be the one starting it off. Richenda stood, hands on hips, in the centre of the lobby, looking up at our efforts. The tree had been placed next to the sweeping staircase so we could reach the higher branches from the stairs. The whole thing sparkled and glittered. Each branch was laden with the finest baubles, some of hand-blown glass, others brightly painted wood, and some intricate half-hollow porcelain affairs with miniature snowy landscapes inside. Amelia clapped her hands in delight. 'Pretsy,' she said. 'Pretsy as Mama.' She cast her mother a sly smile. Even at two pushing three I could tell this one was going to be a handful. Richenda glowed with the compliment and hugged her. 'And well done you. You only broke one bauble.'

Merry, still picking bits of glass out of her hair, did not smile. We had all told Amelia not to attempt to hook decorations on through the stair-rail, but a few minutes' inattention when the three of us were hotly debating whether an angel or a star should go on top of the tree had enabled the naughty sprite to sneak to the top landing clutching the ill-fated bauble. Richenda seemed proud of her daughter's wilfulness. Merry and I foresaw a minx in the making.

Merry departed to thoroughly brush out her hair and consult Merrit on the technical aspects of our operation. Richenda called for Stone and asked him to locate the magic lantern, a novel way of displaying lighted pictures, which she told Stone would delight Amelia. Stone received his orders stoically though I detected from the slight twitch under his eye that the task was less easy than Richenda blithely assumed. Once he had departed I said, 'The attic is rather large, if you remember.'[4] Richenda shrugged. 'It gives him something to do. I have been meaning for ages to get those attics sorted. There's enough space up there to let Amelia have a suite of rooms of her own.'

'She already has some,' I said.

'Not big enough,' said Richenda. 'She needs more space.'

I looked down at the tiny mite. 'At least promise me you won't start on clearing the whole lot out before Christmas.'

Richenda gave me a non-committal smile. She held out her hand to Amelia. 'Let's go and have lunch with Daddy down at the Estate Office,' she said brightly. 'You can get it sent down, can't you, Euphemia?'

'Of course,' I said, knowing Hans would have only ordered sandwiches for himself. I asked the cook to add more of these and some cake to the lunch basket. That should more than suffice. Then I went into the dining room to enjoy a solitary lunch. Much as I liked Amelia, time away from her company was a relief. Richenda was too indulgent, and Merry, who was only a temporary nursery maid, was enjoying the novel experience too thoroughly to discipline the child in the manner it was becoming most clear she needed. If it had been possible, one afternoon with my mother, the estranged daughter of an Earl, would have straightened out Amelia. At least, she had straightened me out. I

---

[4]I was referring to the time we searched the attics for Hans' late wife. A most disturbing occurrence.

suspected Amelia might be more of a challenge even for Mother.

Dinner that night was strained. I do not know precisely what Amelia had done in the Estate Office, but it had taxed even Hans' patience, and he was a man known throughout the business world for never losing his cool. He was a good host over dinner, but I could see his smile was taut on his face and did not reach his eyes. Richenda was also remarkably subdued; although she still ate all of her dinner, she did so with her eyes downcast. Bertram glowered at me, but was taciturnly polite to his hosts. It was not a jolly meal. Amelia, of course, did not join us, but I was sensing that she was going to be as much an obstacle to a jolly Christmas as Bertram's sour mood. I could only hope tonight did not end too disastrously.

I met Merry on the servants' stair around 11 p.m. She giggled nervously as she clutched a candle. Wax dripped onto the stone steps.

'You were right,' she hissed, 'Richenda is much more fun now. This is going to be a great laugh.'

I tugged my shawl more tightly around my shoulders and thought wistfully of my own warm bed. 'I only hope Bertram sees it that way.'

'Oh come on! There's no way we could put him in a worse mood.'

I was spared the necessity of answering this foreboding comment by the arrival of Richenda. She held her candle high, and perilously close to her hair, so we were able to see even at a distance that she was not looking happy. Indeed, her face resembled that of a woman who, expecting to bite into a cake, had found herself biting into a lemon. 'Stone didn't find it,' she said.

Merry gave a *humph* of exasperation. 'Merrit spent ages drilling me.' She saw the look on our faces. 'I told him it was to give Amelia a show. You know how difficult she's being about Father Christmas.'

'Father Christmas?' I said blankly.

'She thinks he'll never find her now she's living here. Gawd, if she could but see the boxes Mr Muller has stacked up in the cupboard downstairs. It's like the whole bleedin' Elves' Workshop has moved in.'

'You can't tell her!' exclaimed Richenda.

'Of course not,' said Merry. 'But she *does* go on about it.'

'I suppose we will need to rethink our plans,' I said, trying not to show how relieved I was. 'Tonight's adventure cannot now take place.'

'Don't be a spoilsport, Euphemia,' protested Merry. 'I'm sure we can do it without it.'

'She's right,' said Richenda, nodding in my general direction and setting her fringe on fire, 'it won't work anywhere near as well.' She was so concerned about making Amelia's first Christmas a happy one that she barely registered she was alight.

I patted Richenda's hair and Merry repositioned her candle. 'You want to get it right, don't you?' she continued barely missing a beat. 'If he guesses it is us straight away there is no point.'

'I suppose so,' said Merry glumly. 'So we give up

105

on the whole idea.'

'Not at all,' said Richenda. 'I shall instruct Stone to look harder. We will reconvene on December the twenty-first. The night of the Solstice. It will be most appropriate.'

I protested, but to no avail. Richenda had once been interested in Spiritualism, but I thought she had long given up on such things. I returned to my bed feeling very like one of Macbeth's witches. What on earth would my dear departed father, the vicar, have said?

Sadly for me, Stone, though almost overwhelmed by Christmas duties, managed to locate the desired object. It was therefore just before midnight on the Solstice that I found myself hiding on the landing with Richenda wrapped in a sheet, Merry clutching the found, and lit, magic lantern, and myself tasked with the unenviable duty of making mysterious noises. After our last attempt I had thought further about my role and obtained a number of items from the kitchen which I hoped would prove more atmospheric than my saying 'Whoo-whoo' and ending up sounding, at best, like a lost owl or a faulty railway engine, neither of these being helpful to the mood we were trying to engender. Merry giggled helplessly. The magic lantern's swirling images jiggled across the passageway's wall.

Richenda stood heavily on her foot. 'You're spoiling the mood. I need to get into character.'

This set Merry off so badly she had to put the lantern down and stuff both her small fists in her mouth to muffle her laughter. Richenda cast her a look of disdain. I found myself biting my lip as she pulled an edge of the sheet up to obscure her face. She gestured to me to open Bertram's bedroom door. As his sister, we had decided Richenda was the only one who could enter his room without impropriety. Besides, if it all went wrong she would be the one left dealing with him. I was fairly sure that Merry, like myself, was ready to bolt and leave her to it if disaster fell. After all, she was the hostess!

Very carefully I tried the knob of Bertram's door. I had the master key with me in case, but the door opened easily. I pushed it wide, my teeth on edge waiting for the hinges to creak, but the housekeeper had instructed her staff well and the door opened without a sound. I moved back, so I was hidden from sight, but not before I had caught a glimpse of a large hump in the bed that stood in the centre of the room. A combined loud snort and snuffle confirmed it was Bertram. Merry slid the magic lantern along the floor and aimed it into the room. I took a quick peek. The effect was most ethereal. Colours swarmed and swam across the room. The white-blue light from the full moon leaking through the curtains only added to the ambience. I hoped the girls were right and that Bertram would believe this to be a dream. He had a weak heart and the last thing we wanted to do was frighten him to death. I began to have strong qualms about the whole project.

Richenda was looking daggers at me through a slit in her sheet so, sighing internally, I gave the box of dry rice I had brought with me a few shakes. The slithering noise of the rice was meant to gently awaken him. Bertram grunted and turned over. I tried a few more times to no effect. I moved on to the cheese grater I had brought and scraped a butter knife over the grill, praying Stone never found out it was I who had damaged his beloved cutlery. 'Thrrup. Thrrup' went the grater. In the quiet and amid the swirling colours I thought it quite effective. I took another peek. Bertram stuck his head under his pillow. Merry looked at me in despair. In desperation I picked up the kitchen pot and rattled around inside it with a metal spoon. The noise seemed incredibly loud. There was a muffled, 'Wot! Wot!' inside the room and the sound of moving bedsheets. I changed back to the rice, not wanting to terrify him. Richenda, taking the sounds as a sign he was now awake, did her best to glide into the room. At least I assume she was aiming for a ghost-like glide. In reality, with her legs pinned by the sheet, she sort of half limped, half hobbled. 'Good Gad!' came Bertram's startled exclamation from the room.

'Yooooooooouuuuu are dreaming-ing-ing,' said Richenda in what she obviously thought was a spectral voice. 'I am the ghost of Christmas …'

Her voice was cut off abruptly, but the sounds of a scuffle. 'What the Dickens!' came Bertram's voice. Merry and I looked at each other. This was it. Time to run.

'Euphemia! Merry!' summoned Bertram's voice.

Too late.

As sheepishly as boot boys summoned before the

butler for a misdemeanour, we popped our heads round the side of the door.

'Can't come in,' said Merry. 'Wouldn't be seemly.'

'Put out that wretched lantern,' snapped Bertram. 'It's giving me a headache.' Obediently, Merry opened the hatch and blew out the candle.

'It were Richenda's idea,' she said, happily throwing her mistress to the wolves – or wolf on this occasion.

'I had thought better of you, Euphemia,' said Bertram. He stood in the middle of the room in his paisley pyjamas, clutching Richenda's sheet. Richenda stood there in a violently coloured orange nightdress that was distinctly honeymoon-like in its style. Bertram seemed finally to take in her attire as he threw the sheet back over her. He shook his head and blinked rapidly as if trying to erase the image. 'Euphemia,' he then continued, 'why didn't you stop them?'

I took a deep breath and said, 'Because I was as fed up as both of them with you ruining our Christmas celebrations.'

'What?' said Bertram staggering back to sit on the bed. 'What are you talking about?'

'Oh you know damn well, Bertram Stapleford, you've been nothing but a bad-tempered grouse since you got here,' said Richenda.

'You 'ave been a bit of a black cloud, sir,' said Merry. 'And we are trying to make it the best Christmas ever for little Amelia. Notwithstanding it's also Mr and Mrs Muller's first Christmas together.'

'But I haven't said a thing,' protested Bertram.

The scales dropped from my eyes. 'Bertram, are you fondly imagining because you haven't broached the topic of whatever is making so disagreeable with any of us that we won't have noticed your black mood?' I asked.

'I've been hiding my feelings,' said Bertram nobly.

'Yeah, right,' said Merry, borrowing from Rory's vocabulary. 'You've been a positive little ray of sunshine.'

'Merry!' I said shocked. 'That's no way to speak to Mr Stapleford.'

'She's absolutely right,' said Richenda. 'You've been a pig, Bertram. A pig to all of us.'

Bertram appealed directly to me. 'Have I?' he asked.

'I am afraid so,' I said.

Bertram stood up. 'Please accept my apologies,' he said. 'Please also accept my assurances that I will alter my behaviour to better fit the season.'

'Just like that?' asked Merry.

'Hadn't you better get back to your charge?' said Bertram. A look passed between Richenda and Bertram.

'Yes,' said Richenda, 'you had better get back to Amelia.'

Merry assumed an expression of disgust, but she knew when she was beaten. She gathered up the magic lantern and stalked off.

'So what is this all about, Bertram?' asked Richenda.

'I would rather not go into details,' said Bertram,

110

'but I have been jilted.'

'What!' said Richenda.

'The Beard Lady,' I said, understanding dawning.

'You were engaged to a woman with a beard?' Richenda's voice climbed higher.

'No. Shhh, Richenda. You'll have the whole house on us,' I said. 'Bertram has been growing his beard because he was told it would give him gravitas.'

'Gravy-what?' said the ever food-conscious Richenda.

'A serious disposition,' said Bertram. 'She wanted me to run for Parliament.'

'But you're about the most apolitical creature I have ever known,' I cried.

'Well, I think you're well shot of her. She can't have any taste if she liked your beard,' said Richenda.

Bertram drew himself up to his full height and attempted an air of great dignity. Something very hard to do in paisley pyjamas. 'My beard was the cause of our parting. She felt it was not sufficient.'

I could not help myself; I giggled. Bertram gave me a hurt look. 'I am sorry, Bertram, but ghastly though your beard is, if a woman truly loved you, I cannot see how that would matter. It is ridiculous.'

'Indeed,' said Richenda. 'No amount of facial foliage would ever make you a good public speaker.'

'Felicity thought I would do rather well,' said Bertram, trying to make a comeback.

'*Felicity*,' said his taunting half-sister, 'is this Felicity deficient in wisdom, years, or both?'

Bertram flushed slightly.

111

'Oh, Bertram,' said Richenda, 'just how old was this girl?'

'Seventeen,' said Bertram muttering into his beard.

'Good heavens,' I said.

'I take it she was very beautiful,' said Richenda.

Bertram sighed and a faraway look came into his eyes, 'She is …' he began, when he was rudely interrupted by Merry, who ran full pelt into the room.

'Amelia,' she panted, 'Amelia's gone!'

As one all the adults in the room transferred their attention to her. Merry began to weep. 'When I left her she was fast asleep. I never shut the nursery door, knowing how Mr Muller fears fire. When I went in to check she was sleeping sound her bed was empty.'

'How long has she been gone?' asked Bertram.

'Dear God!' shrieked Richenda.

'Tell me the window was shut,' I said.

Merry turned to me. 'No, it wasn't. It was only open an inch to stop the room getting stuffy, but it's wider now. You don't think …'

'Is her room on the ground floor?' asked Bertram.

'Of course not,' snapped Richenda. 'But no two-year-old is going to climb out over the roof.'

'She's almost three,' I said. 'And it is not as if the roof seems steep. Well, not at first.'

Bertram snatched up his dressing gown and ran from the room as he struggled to put it on. 'Wake people,' he yelled. Richenda fled. Instinct told me she had gone to find Hans. We needed more practical help. 'Ladders. Gardeners,' I said to Merry. She nodded. She'd been here long enough to know where the head gardener's cottage was. Merry didn't argue; she ran. I headed up to the male corridor, as I knew where the guest valets were housed. I went to wake Rory.

I banged hard on his door. I doubted he was asleep as he opened the door almost at once. By the light of my candle I could see the confusion on his face. 'It's Amelia,' I said at once. 'We fear she has got out onto the roof.'

Rory, who I knew had younger siblings, believed me at once. He stopped only to pick up his coat. He was already wearing slippers. 'Take me to her room,' he said as I had hoped he would. As we hurried along he asked, 'What fool left the window open?'

'Merry,' I said. 'She was sleeping in the room with the child, so I suppose she thought she'd hear if Amelia got up. Only when she came to meet Richenda she did not remember to shut it.'

Rory gave me a look to signify that he knew there was more to the story. 'Honestly,' I protested, 'I had no idea she would leave a window open.'

'She shouldnae have been away from the wean at all.'

'It was only for a few minutes,' I said. I met a look from those luminous green eyes. I dropped my gaze. 'You're right. She should never have been left alone.'

We had reached the nursery door. Rory went in. I followed, hoping against hope that Amelia might simply be hiding under her bed. I bent down to check. Rory cast no more than a cursory eye around the room before he opened the window wider and climbed out. A cold blast of frosty air hit me full in the face. 'Be careful,' I warned. 'Don't slip.'

'I dinnae intend to,' said Rory. 'Could you find a sheet or something, Euphemia? It's guy icy.'

Not entirely sure what he was meaning I took the counterpane off the bed and threw it to him. 'Verra pretty,' said Rory catching it. 'But I was meaning for use as a rope. It's not going to do anyone any guid if I slip and fall on her.'

I stripped the bed in a moment and tied five of the sheets together. I tied one end round the bedpost, knowing I was not strong enough to hold Rory should he slip, and threw the other end to him. He tied it around his waist and moved out.

Rory was now edging out along the flat, almost balcony-like stretch of the roof in front of the window. I peered out. I could see the roof tiles were thick with ice. From somewhere below I heard voices and the noise of a ladder being lifted.

'Bugger,' I heard Rory say. He turned his head back to me. 'I can see her. Wee mite's clinging on half way down the gable.'

Without thinking of the danger I climbed out through the window. 'No,' cried Rory, but it was too late. I crept carefully up beside him. He put a strong arm around my waist. 'She's going to be terrified,' I said. 'You might need me.'

I lay flat along the edge and looked over. Amelia had wedged herself between the gable edge and the wall about half way down. She was shivering with cold. Her little hands were clutched around the side of the gable and her feet pushed hard into the roof tiles to

114

keep her where she was. Her eyes were screwed up shut tight. It was immediately clear that she could not hold herself in that position for much longer and also that she was far too terrified to move.

Bertram's head appeared below us. The ladder did not reach Amelia. It was several feet too short. Bertram continued to climb.

'Stop,' yelled Rory. 'That ladder won't stay balanced if you come any higher. I will get the wean.'

He moved forward slowly. 'Amelia, sweetheart, I am coming to get you.'

The little girl opened her eyes and looked up. 'Santa?' she said.

'Aye, that's me. The Scottish Santa,' said Rory, but even as he reached forward there was the sound of material ripping.

'The rope won't hold,' yelled Bertram and scrambled further up the ladder. Then Rory's words came true. The ladder swayed wildly. Bertram lost his footing. The ladder fell away, but at the last moment Bertram managed to grab the bottom edge of the gable. He hung there. His sleeves fell down and I saw his muscles straining as he tried to hold his weight.

Rory gave his rope a quick tug. Satisfied, he said, 'Hold on, man. I'm coming for you.'

'Get the girl,' commanded Bertram. 'I'm fine.'

Below we could hear sounds of people trying to raise the ladder again. Where was it? I had a sudden fear it had broken in the ice and the cold.

'Santa?' said Amelia. 'I'm so cold.' She reached out a hand towards Rory. Doing this stopped her being wedged in position. Amelia gave a scream as she slid several tiles down the roof. She managed to stop herself from going over the edge by putting her feet against Bertram's face and bracing herself against him.

I saw Bertram's fingers whiten against the edge of the roof. 'I'll get her,' I told Rory. 'You get Bertram.'

'We need another rope,' said Rory.

'There's no time,' I said. 'They'll both be gone any second. Hold onto my feet.'

Rory scowled but nodded. We made our way forward carefully and quickly as far as his makeshift rope would allow. Then I edged forward on my stomach. Rory held onto my ankles. I reached out my arms and found Amelia's waist. She was like a block of ice. I wrapped my arms tightly around her and using all my strength I pulled her towards me. Rory's grip on my ankles tightened. His fingers felt like they were biting into my flesh. I saw the relief on Bertram's face as I started to inch the girl away. His eyes met mine. I realised he could not hold on. I could not reach him without letting go of Amelia. He shook his head very slightly. 'Well done, Euphemia,' he said, and let go.

I did not watch him fall. Inside I concentrated on inching my way back up to Rory and keeping Amelia safe in my arms. Tears coursed down my face.

Rory's arms found me. He pulled us up and back into the nursery. The room was full of people cheering. Amelia was taken from me and wrapped in a blanket. Everything was chaos. I collapsed, sobbing into Rory's arms, and he held me for a long time.

Cold, saddened beyond belief, and overwhelmed by

116

my ordeal I have no clear memory of how I ended up in the dining room downstairs. The large fire was blazing and a mug of something hot had been put into my hands. Stone came and told me quietly that the doctor had been summoned and that Amelia appeared to have taken no hurt from her adventure, though it was possible she might have a chill tomorrow. He patted my hand, something I could never have imagined him doing, and said, 'Well done, Miss St John.' He made no mention of Bertram. Rory had disappeared into the general throng of people milling about. I recognised gardeners and footmen standing side by side drinking soup. This must be the party who had held up the ladder. I wondered who was dealing with Bertram's body when I saw him coming across the room. His eyes sought me out and he hurried over.

'But I saw you fall,' I cried.

Bertram gave a faint smile. 'Thought it was all over for me,' he said. 'But the men over there had gone and got a blanket they held out for me to fall into. Seems no one thought I'd have the strength to hold on for as long as I did. What with that and the snow piled up beneath I'm going to have a lot of bruises ...'

I didn't let him finish. I was out of my chair, my soup flung on the ground as I wrapped my arms around his neck. 'I thought I had lost you,' I sobbed.

'Ow, careful,' said Bertram awkwardly patting my back. 'It's all right, old thing. Bit of an adventure, but we all survived.'

'You were so brave,' I said, my voice muffled against his shoulder.

'You were magnificent,' he said and dropped a kiss on my head before taking my arms from around his body.

There was almost a party atmosphere in the house now the incident was over. It felt like Christmas had come early. We were all giddy with relief. Then Hans walked into the room. I have never seen a man look so angry. We all fell silent. 'Miss St John, Mr Stapleford, I would be grateful if you could join me in my study.'

Bertram made a 'uh-oh' noise under his breath. He took my arm and we followed Hans from the room. Behind us the sounds of merriment ceased and the clearing up began.

Hans' study was a deeply masculine room with a large hearth and wing-backed leather chairs. This evening the fire was cold and no one was sitting. Instead, Richenda was standing awkwardly at the side of the desk, her arm around a weeping Merry, and Rory stood a little apart, his face closed and displaying no emotion. Hans, wearing his glorious green dressing gown, shut the door behind us. 'I am to understand that my wife, Euphemia ,and Merry tried to play a practical joke on you tonight, Bertram, and as a consequence my daughter was left alone in her nursery with the window open.' Merry gave a huge sob. Hans appeared unmoved. His voice was cold and dispassionate. 'My wife assures me she was the leader in this escapade and because of that I can hardly berate the other persons involved. Although I would have thought you, Euphemia, would have had more sense.'

Rory frowned at this. Bertram burst out 'Hang on a

118

minute, Hans …'

Hans put his hand up. 'I am fully aware that Euphemia risked her own life to save my daughter and for that she has my undying gratitude. I have told her before, but I will restate it now in front of witnesses, Euphemia has a place in my household for life.'

Rory's frown vanished.

'I am also aware I owe a deep debt of gratitude to both McLeod and Bertram. That you were obviously willing to give up your life to save my daughter, Bertram, I will never forget. As for your actions, McLeod, I doubt I can ever repay you, but should you ever need anything I can offer - employment, money, reference, even a cottage on my estate, you need only ask. I will be in your debt for the rest of my days.'

Rory ummed and ahhed and looked both embarrassed and pleased. Hans went over and shook him by the hand. It was clear he was thanking him as an equal and not as a servant. I felt tears prick the back of my eyes. Then, finally, he turned to Merry.

He spoke carefully and slowly. I realised he was doing his best to rein in his temper. Merry, must also have sensed his ire, for she was cowering with fright. 'Under the circumstances I must not only dismiss you from my service, but recommend that Sir Richard does the same. I acquit you of deliberate menace, but your negligence cannot go unpunished.'

Richenda began to protest. 'My decision is final,' roared Hans. Everyone in the room started in shock. Hans never raised his voice. Then the master of house turned on his heel and left. Merry collapsed weeping on the floor.

'I'll talk him round,' promised Richenda.

'No offence, ma'am,' said Rory, 'but I think that even you will not be able to move him.'

'Afraid so,' said Bertram.

'But when he's calmed down,' I said. 'He has had the most terrible fright.'

'Would you leave your child with a nursery maid who'd let your child get onto the roof?' asked Rory gruffly in a quiet aside to me.

I sighed. 'No, I would not,' I whispered back, 'but surely Sir Richard will not be dictated to.'

'Business,' said Bertram darkly. 'He won't want to upset Muller. City business.'

The door opened again and we all jumped. ''Cuse me, ma'ams, sirs,' said Merrit, 'I was looking for Merry.'

Bertram stepped aside allowing him to see Merry. Merrit went forward, crouched down and embraced his girlfriend. 'Ah, pet, no one thinks you did it deliberate,' he said. 'The little one is fine. There's no need to cry.'

'But I don't have a position,' sobbed Merry. 'I'm homeless.'

Merrit turned his head to look at Bertram. 'Could I tell her tonight, sir? I know you wanted me to do it on Christmas Day …'

'Yes, dammit, man,' said Bertram. 'I'd been wondering when you would show up.'

Ignoring the rest of us, Merrit placed a finger under her chin and turned Merry's face up to his.

'Sweetheart,' he said, 'Mr Bertram has been so kind as to give me a cottage seeing as I'm his chauffeur. A cottage for life.'

'That's nice,' said Merry in a wobbling voice.

'It's even got a patch of garden for growing veggies. It's not a cottage for one,' spelled out Merrit, 'it's a family house.'

Merry looked at him blankly.

'My dearest Merry, will you do me the honour of becoming my wife and living with me in my cottage?'

Merry threw a look at Bertram. 'That was the point of giving him the cottage,' said Bertram.

Merry looked puzzled for a moment, as if she could not believe what she was hearing, then she broke into a huge smile. 'Yes, oh yes, Merrit,' she said. 'Of course I'll marry you.'

'This is certainly turning out to be one memorable Christmas,' said Bertram in my ear. 'If I promise to behave, Euphemia, do you think we could get through the rest of the festive season without any more adventures?'

'Oh, heavens, I do hope so,' I said.

'Merry Christmas,' said Rory to the newly engaged pair. 'And congratulations.'

Richenda clapped her hands. 'Merry Christmas, everyone!' she said. 'Now, who wants some celebratory cake?'

Merry Christmas Everybody

Jane Risdon

The track faded and no-one spoke; the only sound came from the creak of the recording engineer's chair as it thudded upright from its reclined position where he had been leaning back, eyes closed, listening hard to the rough mix from the night before.

The others in the room jumped at the sudden noise but their eyes never left the huge monitors above the desk. At last Jonty, band leader and lead guitarist said, 'So you're saying you haven't been messing around with the track and you're not having us on; right, Buff?' He walked to the mixing desk and turned, resting against the leather padding, unlit cigarette hanging from the corner of his mouth. He crossed his long thin legs. 'So, like, what's the deal then?'

Buff swivelled his chair to face the rest of Twister, who were seated along the back of the studio wall, mugs of tea untouched. He glared at them, finally focusing on Gary. 'I told you, I don't know. I can't explain it. I haven't touched the mix since we finished last night and as far as I know, no-one else has been in here. Unless one of you is responsible – playing silly buggers – sodding time-wasting wind-up merchant.'

Gary, the bass player, who didn't want Buff working on the tracks in the first place, shook his head angrily and pointed at Buff. 'Look mate, there's keyboards all over that track and none of us put 'em there so it's bleedin' obvious who did. I fuckin' knew you'd turn us into fuckin' Night Ranger given half the chance.'

Buff gave him the finger.

'Shut the fuck up, all of you.' Twister's manager,

Tristram Guinness, held up his hands. The bad feeling between Buff and Gary was beginning to really piss him off and try his patience. 'No-one is accusing anyone. But the fact is there are keyboards on the track which shouldn't, and couldn't, be there unless someone played them and recorded them. Time's money and whoever it was better get the message; this crap stops now!'

He walked out slamming the studio door, causing the Christmas decorations in the corner of the room to flutter and shimmy.

'Time's bloody money,' mimicked Jet. 'So, who did it then? He's gone, so cough up.' Never without his sticks in his hands he tapped a rhythm on his knees. The last few days recording had turned into a nightmare, he hated atmospheres and this one was getting more toxic by the day.

The band looked from one to the other, Buff shook his head exasperated. 'I'm gonna say this once only – next fucker messes with my desk and my mix is dead! Get it?'

He turned back to the desk hitting the replay button, listened for a while, and then pressed a few more buttons, wiping the phantom keyboard track from the recording.

'OK, here we go, listen up.' Buff put the track back up on the desk and hit play again. This time the original recording from the night before, minus the phantom keyboard parts, belted out from the monitors on the wall and on the desk. The band gathered round to listen and comment on their own parts, and the track

124

in general, which was what they had been doing when the offending keyboards suddenly appeared on the recording. There was no way they'd ever allow keyboards on their material; not ever.

'I'm going to re-do my lead on this track,' said Jonty. 'I came up with a much better lead break when I was in in bed last night; got to try it, Buff.' He picked up his guitar and played the piece he wanted to re-record. When everyone agreed it was better Buff brought the track back up on the desk with the drums and bass, but minus Jonty's former contribution. Jonty plugged his guitar into the desk and began to play.

After several takes and some over-dubbing with guitar effects, everyone was pleased with the new guitar parts and Kris, the rhythm guitarist, re-did some of his parts to fit with Jonty's. The track sounded full and gutsy; once the vocals had been recorded, Buff would decide if the track needed anything else added to fatten it up. But it was beginning to seriously rock already.

'Where's Alex, by the way?' The lead singer was never around when the tracks were being laid, but always first to complain if something wasn't to his liking. 'Still in bed?' Buff looked up from the desk.

'Yeah something like that,' laughed Gary, who'd seen a leggy blonde going into Alex's room the night before. The band exchanged knowing looks behind Buff's back. Girls were strictly off-limits during recording. Tristram would go mental if he knew what Alex was up to. 'Do you need him yet?'

'Nope, it's cool. Just make sure he's wide awake

and sober later this afternoon in case I'm ready.' Buff bent over the desk, pressed play and began to clean up the track.

The band left Buff to tidy the track and add some effects and more over-dubs while they headed down the local pub. 'Good riddance,' he muttered as the last one left the studio, 'little shits enjoy a little too much Christmas spirit for their own good,' Buff said to Geoff, his second engineer. Geoff nodded and carried on prepping the live room.

When Tristram asked Buff to record and produce Twister, he'd agreed reluctantly – Buff wasn't a huge fan of the band. Pressure from his own manager and the band's record company, plus the fact that royalties were slow coming in from his last project which had taken almost a year to produce, eventually swayed him; he needed the money. 'Yeah, they write cool lyrics, it's not that, Tristram, it's just the whole vibe they put out and their music doesn't do it for me,' he told Tristram for the umpteenth time. 'I like Jonty, he's cool, but the rest of them do my head in. No-one wants to touch them, Tristram, you know that. They're bloody toxic.'

'I know, mate, but they're creative beings, you know what that's like.' Tristram knew just how Buff felt, he'd almost jacked it in with the band many times but things were lean for his management company as well and having spent a bucket load of his own money, still un-recouped, getting the band off the ground during the last five years he couldn't afford to walk. Not yet at any rate. 'I can make it worth your while, an extra percent on producer royalties – how about it?

'Well, all right then, but you'd better have a serious word with those wankers and make sure they get their heads in gear. First fuck-up and I walk. I mean it.' Buff heard the band were a nightmare in the studio; the producer on their last two albums had refused to work with them again, that was serious. 'I don't have Buddy's patience, any shit goes on and that's it. How he stuck it for two records I don't know.'

Later that night the band gathered in the studio ready to listen to Alex lay his vocal parts on the now almost complete track. 'Only another nine more to record,' thought Buff as he watched Geoff prepare the mic for Alex. 'Deep bloody joy.'

Once everyone was settled and Alex was behind the mic in the vocal booth, the lights dimmed. He put his cans on and gave the thumbs up that he could hear Buff. 'Gonna run the track through once, just to give you the feel. I've made some changes since last night as you know, and I wanna be sure you're familiar. Don't sing yet. Ready.' Buff pressed play and the guitar intro started. Alex nodded his approval of the changes Jonty had made, and closed his eyes, concentrating.

'What the fuck?' he shouted into the mic as a keyboard started playing on the chorus and middle eight. 'I thought we told you to cut that shit out.' He stormed out of the booth and into the control room, his face puce with rage. 'I oughta smack your fuckin' face in, you tosser,' punching a stunned Buff on the shoulder.

Jonty jumped up and pulled Alex off the producer, whose chair had smashed into the bank of keyboards and effects modules on the other side of the room. 'I'll fuckin' kill you if you lay another fuckin' finger on me; you better believe it.' Buff shouted, inspecting the gear for damage. 'Any damage and you pay for it, get me?'

'Knew this was a bleedin' mistake, he couldn't produce a fuckin' turd,' yelled Gary.

'No? Well I sure as hell am trying my best to produce one from you bastards,' Buff yelled back, spittle dripping down his chin.

Tristram, who had gone outside to make a phone call, came in just as Alex was about to go for Buff again and shouted, 'What the hell's going on now? It's worse that a kindergarten full of bloody toddlers; can't leave you alone for one minute.'

'Trust you to be missing when the shit hits the fan,' Buff shouted. 'You keep that arsehole out of my face or I'll re-arrange his for him.' He pointed at Alex.

'Let's calm down, for fuck's sake,' shouted Kris, 'This ain't helping.' His eyes pleaded with Jet to do something. Jet jumped up and hit the tambourine which he'd been messing around with. Everyone froze. 'Right, let's all sit down and shut the fuck up.'

'OK, now what's going on here?' Tristram sat on the arm of the longest sofa and waited. No-one said anything for a few moments as Buff and Alex continued to glare at each other and Gary eventually lowered his fist. Buff had no idea how close he'd been to having his face smashed in, Gary fumed silently to himself; he was going to get that bastard as soon as the album was finished.

'Some bugger's been messin' with the tracks again. More fuckin' keyboards all over them. I can't understand it. I haven't left the studio all day except for the loo and Geoff has been in here all that time as well, though he did go for coffee and Chinese for us both, but dunno what time that was.' He pointed to his long-time second engineercum studio tech. , who was looping yards of electric cable, then hanging the loops on the pegs in the store room just off the main live room. They could see him through the glass which separated the control room from the three live rooms.

'Are you sayin' no-one's been in here all day or evening except you two?' Jonty pursed his full lips and shook his head. 'How the hell did the keys get on the track? Are you re-using old tape that's not been wiped?'

Buff gave him a look of contempt and said, 'I never re-use tape and few people ever do, so you can *wipe* that idea outta your head now.' Buff scratched his head and bent over the desk. He pressed play again and sat back in his chair, headphones covering one ear. 'Listen to this and tell me how it got there.'

The men stood behind him as Buff moved the faders on the desk and the track started from the beginning. He turned the volume up and sent the track through the monitors. Geoff came back into the studio having witnessed the aggression as he worked the other side of the glass. 'What's going on?' he asked Kris and everyone hissed, 'Shush!'

129

Just as the chorus started, a keyboard cut in over the top of Jonty's lead and almost drowned it out. It was louder and more aggressive than before and as the band listened they realised it was playing a completely different melody to that of the lead guitar.

'Why would anyone put keys on which aren't even playing the same bloody tune?' Tristram asked Buff. 'I mean it sounds like something else, I can't put my finger on it, but don't you think it sounds sort of familiar?'

Everyone got closer to the desk and Buff pressed rewind and played the track again. 'Yes, there!' said Tristram. 'That part coming next. I've heard that somewhere before. Anyone know it?' No-one seemed to recognise it, though Jet looked thoughtful, but he kept his mouth shut. What he was thinking was just too 'out there.'

'I don't fuckin' care what it does or doesn't sound like,' shouted Buff. 'It shouldn't be on the bloody track. It's NOT an old tape and no-one has touched this desk except me, all day.'

'Drop everything out and leave the keys,' said Tristram. 'Let's hear it on its own.'

'Am I doin' my fuckin' vocals tonight or what?' Alex moaned. Alex and his girl had plans for later and if he didn't get back before the housekeeper at the manor house attached to the studio knocked off they wouldn't be getting anything to eat 'I mean, if you guys don't need me I might as well ...'

Before he could finish, Tristram said, without turning to look at him, 'You stay as long as we stay and you can forget the girl. I sent her packing just after you decided to show your face.' Alex looked shocked and he wondered if Buff or Gary had seen the girl and shopped him, but Tristram said, 'Don't go looking to blame someone else, I saw you sneaking her in last night. I'll deal with you later.'

Kris and Jet laughed out loud and did the thumbs down sign to Alex, pulling faces at him behind Tristram's back. 'Grow the fuck up, you two,' Tristram said, sensing them pantomiming behind him. 'Time's money and this is wasting a ton of it.' The band rolled their eyes at hearing their manager's mantra yet again.

'We've got A&R here next week to hear what we've come up with so far,' said Tristram. 'Guys, we need this done so the label can see how we're spending their dosh.'

The track played again and everyone listened hard. Jet looked across at Jonty, wondering if he was thinking the same as he was; the unthinkable. The keyboard seemed to play a melody of its own which Jet knew he'd heard before, a long time ago, but he tried put the thought out of his head. 'Got to go for a slash,' he said and left the room before anyone could reply.

Jet could hear the blood rushing in his ears as he went to the crate of beers in the corner of the kitchen. He picked out a can and opened it, almost throwing the warm liquid down his throat. He opened the door to the kitchen garden, lit a cigarette, and leaned against the wall smoking, drinking, and trying not to think.

'You all right, mate?' Jet turned as Jonty joined him for a smoke; beer in hand, they gazed up at the star-filled sky. Jet didn't answer, watching as a satellite passed overhead. They both watched it in silence for a while and then Jonty said, 'You coming back inside? Tristram thinks we should all get on and forget the keys. He thinks one of us is prating around and when he finds out who, he said he is seriously thinking of kicking them out of the band.'

'It's no-one in the band, Jonty, at least not now,' said Jet, stubbing his smoke out on the ground. He looked at Jonty who just shook his head, he avoided looking at Jet.

'Mate, don't even think it; it's nuts. Stuff like that'll do your head in.' He downed the rest of his can and threw his cigarette end on the lawn. 'Let's go back in before our lord and master throws a wobbly.' Jonty patted his old schoolmate on the shoulder and headed back to the studio. Jet came in on his heels.

'Meeting of the bloody Girl Guides out there, was it?' asked Tristram as they came back into the control room. 'Going to the loo in pairs now, are we?' The rest of the band roared with laughter. Geoff and Buff rolled their eyes and waited.

'Right, so what do you make of it?' Buff asked his fellow listeners. 'Sounds like a Fender Rhodes to me, and the person playing it certainly knows his stuff. The piece is good, it's just not right for this track. Anyone here play keys, apart from me that is?'

'Buff, they're all multi-instrumentalists, of course they play keys, but look at their faces, mate, they're as baffled as I am – and if you didn't put the keys on and they didn't, then who did?' said Tristram, lighting a cigarette and blowing the smoke out in circles.

'Well, don't look at me,' said Geoff hurriedly, 'I can play, but I didn't do it, why would I?'

He shifted his gaze to Buff. 'I've got another gig in studio 3 when your album's done so I can't afford all this time-wasting. I'm engineering the new Spikes album, so playing silly buggers here isn't going to help me if things get held back.' Geoff looked at the band. 'Besides, when would I've been able to do it, the place is either busy or locked down like a nun's knickers?' The band fell about laughing. 'Buff keeps the keys.'

'Look this isn't getting us anywhere, I can't explain any of it. We need to get on, the budget won't run to lost hours and days while we try and figure this shit out,' said Tristram. 'Buff, clean the track, again, and let's get Alex's vocals down ASAP.' He sat on the leather sofa, opened the NME and started reading; in the back of his mind he kept wondering where he'd heard that keyboard melody before.

Alex managed to get his vocals down in two takes, which was a relief to Buff who was feeling exhausted. 'I'll leave the track as it is and we can listen again in the morning and see what else needs doing to the vocals. I might add some reverb, I'll see.' He gathered up his notes and headed for the door. 'Come on, out!' he said firmly, 'I'm locking up – you can all see me do it – and I'm giving Tristram the keys; he can open up in the morning.'

Everyone followed him out. Geoff had already left

as he wanted to see a mate's band playing at a local club. 'It's a gig to raise money for a local hospice; want to come?' he asked the others. 'They do it every Christmas since my mate's mum died in there.'

'Off to bed; alone,' said Tristram.   Make sure you're all here at nine tomorrow; time's money and we're losing shed loads messing around with bloody phantoms.' Twister rolled their eyes and Buff turned off the lights, Tristram locked-up and followed the band over to the manor house complex where they all had rooms for the duration of recording – part of the 'all-in' package Tristram had negotiated at the world famous studio, which the record company agreed to pay for, all recoupable of course.

This album was proving to be more expensive than the other two Twister had recorded, even though recording was taking place in England. Even taking into consideration the savings made by not paying additional costs for flights, visas, and work permits, shipping their own gear, and accommodation costs for the band and their crew, it still worked out more expensive because much more time had been allowed for the project than before – and Buff didn't come cheap.

Buff usually kept his financial woes to himself. In spite of being a much sought after producer with a superstar profile and reputation, thus commanding huge fees, the time it took for royalties to filter through from around the world made planning his life difficult. His last divorce had cost him dear. 'I'm only taking this gig to ensure I can cover the amount that bitch

Carrie screwed out of me,' he confided in Geoff when they discussed taking the project. Geoff had been his engineer for years and the two made a formidable team.

'Let's go for it,' Geoff agreed reluctantly; he didn't much care for Twister as people, let alone their music. 'Besides, if we turn them down it won't do us much good with the label for future gigs,' he added wisely.

'It just feels weird,' Buff told Geoff before he signed the producer contract with Tristram, 'you know I won't touch anything I don't totally get; but needs must as they say.' They played the band's albums over and over trying to get a handle on them, and what Buff especially, could do for them. 'I'll do it and it will be fucking amazing, but this is the first time I've accepted something I can't get into.'

'It sucks,' said Geoff, silently rejoicing in being single.

Tristram and the record company wanted a bigger global hit this time with millions more sales and Buff's name on the record would help achieve it. Usually Geoff would do the hands-on engineering and Buff, as producer, would instruct and over-see the laying down of the tracks, deciding and directing what went on the tracks, and how; ensuring that the band 'sounded' like themselves, enhanced and marketable to the record company – they were paying so they had to get what they wanted – it also had to be acceptable to radio. If radio didn't like the finished mixes they might refuse to play the record or demand additional and different mixes; costing more ultimately.

'I've produced multi-platinum albums for dozens of bands, as you know,' he told Tristram, 'and I can and will do it for Twister.'

Buff had to have vision; he had to get magic out of the band's performance and on to the record. He was responsible for achieving the main mixes and the tracks ready for final mixes – done elsewhere by a different mix engineer – and eventual mastering, again done by another engineer at a mastering lab. Buff had to work magic; he had to get that magic from the band and translate that into a hit record.

'Yeah, we're bloody magicians,' laughed Geoff.

The following morning Tristram opened up the studio and switched the lights on, dimming them to an acceptable working level. The decorations shimmered, creating a cosy atmosphere – for now. He went to the desk, hit play, and settled back in Buff's chair, sipping his coffee and waiting for the track to run. He almost choked when the chorus kicked in. Alongside Alex's vocal he could hear another voice, singing a completely different melody line and it wasn't Alex. 'What the fuck?' he whispered. The hairs on the back of his neck and arms tingled as the high pitched ethereal vocal drifted across Alex's gutsy rock voice.

'Who's that you got on my vocal?' demanded Alex who for once had managed to rouse himself before lunchtime. 'What the hell's going on? You trying to push me out, is that it?'

His manager glared at him, 'Listen, you big girl's blouse.' Tristram pointed to the monitors, 'Who is that? I know that voice, I just can't make it out.' He

136

turned back to the desk and hit rewind and then play. The voice drifted over the chorus and in the background a bit lower in the mix, a keyboard was playing a different melody again.

'Shit!' Alex shook his head. 'Those bloody keys are still in there. I'll fuckin' smack Buff. He's such a liar, 'I've taken them off,' yeah, right off by the sounds of it.'

'Alex, will you put a sock in it before I smack you one!' shouted Tristram. 'Listen and try keeping your mouth shut and your ears open for a change.' There was something so familiar about the melody the keys were playing and yet he couldn't quite drag it from the depths of his memory. Something about that vocal too ... what the hell was it? He kept hitting replay and listening hard. Alex sulked on the sofa, bored with the whole keyboard thing and really pissed off after the dressing down he'd got the night before over the girl in his room. Tristram was far from his favourite person this morning, and now this with the vocals.

Buff and Geoff came in drinking coffee, with packets of sandwiches for their mid-morning snack. Tristram glanced at them and said, 'Here, listen to this.' And pressed play.

Buff froze for a moment before he yelled, 'Right, that's it, I've fuckin' had enough of this shit. I don't care who did it or why, but I want the arsehole out of my studio or I'll quit. You can replace the prick with a session guy, whoever, I don't give a toss, but I don't want to hear the shit again. Got it?' And he stormed out of the studio, bumping into the rest of Twister as they came in. Geoff remained in the studio, not sure what to do. Some Christmas Eve this was turning into.

'What the hell is up with him?' asked Kris, concern in his eyes. This whole gig was turning into a fucking nightmare; so much tension. 'I wish everyone'd just chill.'

'But this is crazy,' said Gary after they'd listened to the track a dozen times, 'If you had the studio key, Tristram, what's going on? Who is that on there?'

Geoff couldn't wait to hear this 'Yes, what the hell is going on, guys?' He needed to know in case Buff asked him what went down after he'd left. 'Buff will walk if this isn't sorted out now.'

Jet and Jonty exchanged looks. They'd decided the night before that if anything else 'fuckin' weird,' happened again they'd tell what they knew; or at least what they thought they knew. Jonty nodded to Jet, 'Go on, you tell them.'

Before he could say another word Alex leapt across the room and grabbed Jet around the throat, 'It's you, you did it, you fuckin' tosser,' Jonty and Kris tried to pull him off Jet, but not before Gary had chance to take a swipe at Jet too. 'I'll kill you, you bastard. You never wanted me in the band, I know you think your stupid idiot of a brother is better than me.' Alex yelled, kicking out at Jonty and Kris and managing to bash Gary in the mouth with his elbow. 'This is a trick to get him in and me out.'

'You shut your mouth,' shouted Jet. 'You shit-for-brains prick.' He lashed out at Alex and caught Jonty's fingers by mistake. 'My brother's happy with his own band.'

Jonty winced and Tristram shouted 'Fire!' and everyone stopped dead. Tristram hadn't moved from Buff's chair the whole time; the penny had just dropped. The studio went silent except for their laboured breathing. Suddenly the lights flickered and it went dark for a few seconds. 'Shit, what the hell …?' Geoff didn't finish. The track started playing as the lights came back on, brighter than before.

'Turn that off,' shouted Jet, extricating himself from his bandmates who were still all over him. 'Tristram, turn that shit off.'

'I didn't put the bugger on,' Tristram said slowly. 'It just came on. I didn't touch it.'

Geoff walked to the desk and pressed the button but the track didn't stop. It got louder and louder until the monitors were jumping off the desk and walls with vibration. 'It won't work; button's stuck I think,' he yelled as the band gathered behind their manager who was staring at the monitors, his face tight, his brain fuzzy, his thoughts muddled.

The track grew louder and louder as Geoff and Tristram pressed buttons, slid flying faders, doing everything they could think of to stop the track. The keyboards drowned out the rest of the instruments on the track and the phantom vocal sat right on top of Alex's.

'Listen, listen to the vocals,' shouted Jonty, 'I know who it is; Tristram, Jet, listen up.'

'I said let's not go there,' Jet yelled over the top of the track. 'It's crazy.'

'No, he's right, it is, it's him all right, no bleedin' doubt.' Tristram shook his greying hair in disbelief. 'Penny dropped earlier, but I can't get my head round it, it's, it's bloody insane.'

'Look I can't shut the fucker up, let's go outside and I'll get Buff,' Geoff opened the studio door and everyone followed him out. 'Can't bloody think straight in there.'

The large kitchen area provided relief from the racket in the studio, the doors sound-proofed and sturdy. They sat at the long wooden table smoking, drinking coffee, and eating mince pies sent over from the housekeeper in the main house. Geoff had gone in search of Buff.

'So, is anyone gonna spill or what?' asked Kris, deeply disturbed by what he'd witnessed in the studio. 'Seems you lot know something Gary, Alex, and me don't.'

'Yeah, we do, mate,' said Jonty slowly, 'but let's see if Geoff finds Buff first and then you'll know.' He picked at his mince pie; his chest was so tight he felt he'd explode. 'Wait a bit longer, agreed?' He looked at Tristram and Jet. Both nodded, their faces white and troubled.

'Some bloody Christmas this is,' said Gary miserably. 'Looks like we're gonna be here tomorrow after-all. Can't see us getting a day off now, not after all this crap.'

'We're all away from our friends and family Gary, not just you,' Tristram said bitterly. 'This is the fifth year running that I've been away for Christmas, thanks to you guys.'

'Us?' Alex shouted, 'No-one makes you work over Christmas, you wanker, your choice, mate, yours not ours.' He thumped the table hard.

'No, he's right,' said Tristram as Jet and Jonty were about to remonstrate with their band mates. 'I decided to take your guys on, to try and break the band in the US and Asia, I was aware it meant working hard for five or six years. It has to be done. I can't dictate to the label or radio, or miss opportunities for touring so I can be at home, any more than you can. We have to go where the music takes us and if that means missing holidays and Christmas, well, my wife for one understands. She doesn't like it, the kids hate it, but we agreed a long time ago.'

'Look, mate, we all appreciate what you and your family does for us, we do, seriously,' said Jet, feeling bad at the attitude and ingratitude shown by Alex and the others. 'We don't have wives and kids, it's no skin – really it's not.' Jonty and Kris nodded. Alex glared.

Buff walked in looking murderous. 'What's this with the track not cutting?' he asked Tristram who stood, ready to go back into the studio. 'You lot stay put. Tristram, Geoff, follow me.'

They left the band looking sullen and pissed off. As they opened the studio door the noise levels were in danger of blowing the speakers and their ears. Buff ran to the desk and pressed the buttons. He didn't want to pull the plug on the desk before backing up everything on to another track. Normally he'd have done it before leaving the studio, but, given the way he'd left, he hadn't. Geoff handed out earplugs but the noise was still audible. The monitors were jumping as the bass and drums vibrated. The vocal was at screaming pitch and then suddenly everything stopped.

'What did you do?' Tristram asked Buff.

'Nothing mate, I wasn't touching the desk just then.' He looked at Geoff.

'Nope, me neither.' Geoff shook his head. He looked confused and bit his bottom lip. 'Just stopped.'

A looked passed between Jonty and Jet as the studio door closed. They both noticed that Kris, Gary, and Alex were intent upon their coffee and mince pies, bemoaning the fact that it was Christmas Day tomorrow and they were stuck in the studio.

'Some bloody festive season this is,' Gary said. 'Buff was a serious mistake for this album, I don't care how the stuff got on the track; he is responsible.' He picked the berries off of a holly decoration placed in the centre of the table and threw them across the kitchen. Jonty nodded at Jet and they slipped into the studio. The noise stopped and the lights flickered on and off just as they closed the door behind them.

'What the hell ...?' Tristram's voice sounded tight and dry as the studio lights grew bright again before they were once again plunged into total darkness. Gradually the live room began to shimmer and pulsate with bright white light. It filled every corner and nook and cranny. It appeared to emanate from a spot just in front of the mic stand where it was brighter and more translucent. No-one spoke as Tristram's voice trailed off. He stared agog at the spectacle unfolding before them. The control room, normally in constant need of air-conditioning, seemed to develop a slight breeze starting around shoulder level, yet it didn't feel like the AC – it was freezing cold. The men shivered and held their breath as the desk lit up and all the faders began to move up and down as if an engineer was operating them. The monitors hissed with white noise for a few seconds and then the phantom keyboardist began to play the now familiar melody, solo, without the other instruments.

'I knew it,' whispered Jet, 'I bloody knew it as soon as I heard it the first time.'

'What did you know?' Buff sounded annoyed, not scared like Jet.

'I think we know who is messing with the tracks, Buff,' croaked Tristram, finding his voice again. 'We three know.'

All of a sudden the music stopped and a voice that sounded not unlike Slade's Noddy Holder screamed 'Merry Christmas.' Buff nearly jumped out of his Spanish leather cowboy boots. 'What the fuck?'

The studio door burst open and the rest of the band tramped in, unaware of the drama unfolding in front of the others. 'Pub time, let's bugger off down the ....' Alex's voice was drowned out by the screaming voice repeating 'Merry Christmas.' Each time louder and more aggressively.

Everyone gaped at the desk and monitors, unable to comprehend what was happening. Buff frantically pushed buttons, rode the faders, and eventually Geoff went behind the desk, got underneath it, and fiddled with the Spaghetti Junction of wiring there. He yanked a handful of wires out and the monitors and their channels went dead on the desk; silence.

'What the hell's that all about?' Alex looked horrified. Kris and Gary wore similar expressions. Tristram pointed to the door. 'Follow me. I need a drink.'

The public bar of The Highwayman was still not full to capacity so they were soon all seated in the snug with their drinks, away from the office colleagues and shop workers having a last lunchtime drink to celebrate Christmas Eve, before heading home to undertake last minute chores for the big day. Bing Crosby was doing his thing with 'White Christmas,' again.

Jonty and Jet sipped silently, conscious of what was about to be revealed and feeling very uncomfortable. Tristram cleared his throat and gazed at Twister, Buff, and Geoff, wondering how to begin. 'Well, it's been … I mean it's … what you should know is …' but he couldn't voice what he needed to say. His eyes pleaded across the table where he met Jonty's troubled gaze. Jonty nodded reluctantly.

'What Tristram wants to tell you, what you need to know is that we know who's doing this.' He took a long pull on his beer and wiped his hand across his mouth. 'We think.'

'I'll kill the bugger when I get hold of him,' hissed Buff, 'bloody messing with my sessions, it's not on.' Geoff nodded agreement; he'd like a go at the bastard

144

too.

'You'd have a job mate,' said Jet. 'He's already dead.' His band mates exchanged looks, not sure what to make of Jet's statement. 'Seriously, I kid you not,' Jet added solemnly.

'Yeah right,' Gary sniggered. 'Bloody ghosts and ghouls, is that it?' and he nudged Alex, spilling some of his drink.

'Shut up you prat.' Jonty jabbed his finger angrily at Gary. Gary took a large drag on his cigarette but didn't respond for a change.

'Please, just listen for once,' Tristram snapped. 'It's important.'

'Way back when Jet and I first got the band together, when we were still at school, we had a keyboard player, Danny – a mate since we were little. We played school dances and at youth club. Then the three of us used to do local pubs when we left school.' Jonty smiled sadly. 'We couldn't get a decent drummer back then, we used a drum machine and sometimes Danny played bass.'

'Bloody closet Night Ranger, I might've guessed. You did West Coast crap I bet!' laughed Gary.

'Anyway,' continued Jonty, throwing Gary a filthy look. 'We did really well, got a large following, and we had a bit of a buzz going, so we sent a demo tape out to the labels in London, just testing the water really.'

'Yeah, at first nothing happened, just the usual 'thanks but no thanks,' but we carried on,' said Jonty. 'Anyway, after about six months we managed to get a gig on Radio One Rock Wars and we went down to Maida Vale to the Radio One studios to record a session with a proper producer.' Jonty smiled at the memory. 'We'd found a really heavy drummer by then, Mike, and we had a really hard vibe going ... except for the keyboards.'

'Yeah, we had a ball, it was amazing. We were in a professional studio instead of a crummy semi-pro set-up in a mate's garage. It was awesome,' said Jet, his eyes bright with excitement.

'Right, so what's this gotta do with the crap on our tracks?' Alex was not known for his patience and this was beginning to do his head in. 'If we're not recording today I want to go and see the missus. It's bloody Christmas in case you've forgotten.'

'You're not going anywhere; we're recording today, tomorrow, and for the rest of the six weeks, so shut it,' Tristram said through gritted teeth.

'That remains to be seen,' Buff said. He hadn't yet decided to carry on . 'Taking a lot for granted aren't you?'

'Hear Jonty out, then we'll see what we can sort,' Tristram said.

'Come on mate, spill.' Kris wanted to know more.

Before Jonty could continue they were joined by a woman dressed in a Salvation Army uniform. She shook a container covered in fake holly and tinsel at the men and waited; smiling widely. They all searched their pockets and deposited their loose change in the container. 'Bless you all, Merry Christmas, everybody,' she said and moved to a group of giggling women drinking Babycham, eating crisps, and singing along with 'I saw Mommy Kissing Santa Claus,' which someone had put on the jukebox.

'As I was saying,' Jonty sighed loudly. 'We did the session and it went on air three weeks later. It was mad. We got loads of calls from labels all wanting to sign us, you know how it is.' He looked at his beer. 'Before the session we couldn't get arrested, then everyone and his uncle was after us.' Jet and Buff nodded, they knew how it went.

'We saw lots of labels, played showcases for them all, and got loads of feedback about the songs, the way we looked, and what they thought we should be like. That's how it is.' Jet watched his band mates nodding their agreement. 'Some wanted us harder, more like Sabbath, and others thought we should go more AOR, with a softer image. It was a friggin' nightmare trying to resist the pressure to change.' Jet ran his hands through his long dark hair. 'We were auditioning bass players too and that was going nowhere fast.'

'We had loads of managers trying to get us to sign with them and they all had their ideas as well, about our sound, image, and who was good for the band and who wasn't,' Jonty added. 'We had a massive row with Danny, he wanted to play keyboards not bass, and he wanted to go with A&M records because they had a guy they wanted to manage us – can't recall his name – but he was an arsehole.'

'Yeah, they did a number on him, filling his head with crap about living in LA, having a condo on the beach and half-naked models dripping around his own pool.' Jet shook his head. 'He was sold good and proper. He kept on and on about how we could make a fortune and he'd always dreamed about living on the West Coast, having the red Corvette, the whole nine yards. We didn't want that, Jonty and me. We're about the integrity of our music, not just the bloody babes and dosh; we're metal through and through.'

'In the end we had a fight. Bloody horrid it was, real fists and violent.' Jet shuddered. 'Danny got pissed off his head and phoned the guy from A&M and spilled his guts to him. Well, that was a mistake. They told him they wouldn't touch a band who weren't one hundred percent into the deal or the manager they offered. They didn't want Danny on his own either.'

'It was coming up to Christmas and the labels were closing down for the holidays so they wanted us to commit. Sony and BMG in London kept the pressure up but Jet and I liked the sound of Zomba. They had bands like us and good American distribution and we'd showcased for a manager who had managed successful bands, just like us, on their label.' He glanced at Tristram. 'We liked him and felt he would be good for us. Danny hit the booze and he cocked up the second showcase we were asked to do for him.' Jonty looked at Tristram who was frowning into his beer. Suddenly he realised no-one was talking and he looked up. All eyes were on him.

'Yeah, I wasn't impressed with him or his attitude at the time; anyway, I knew we could find someone else who could also write songs with the others. I didn't think the band needed keyboards anyway, it wasn't adding anything to the sound and I knew I could market them without. Their sound was harder and more aggressive than the AOR direction Danny wanted to go.'

Tristram took a deep breath before continuing. 'I told Zomba Danny would hold the band back – I could make a success of them – without Danny.' He looked uncomfortable for a moment, then said in a stronger voice, 'I was right. Keyboards took them in the wrong direction.'

'Yeah, and then Mike got cold feet. His dad wanted him to get a job and have some stability, plus he was planning on getting engaged to – what's her face – and save for a house,' Jet added, 'So right at the worst possible time, he left the band.' Jet looked angry.

'Bloody painter and decorator last I heard with loads of kids, living in a council house near his dad.' Jonty added shaking his head at the memory. 'What a prat!'

'We hadn't decided upon a bass player and suddenly we had to find another drummer. It sucked,' said Jet. 'Danny didn't want to play bass.'

'Anyway, to cut a long story short and all that, I negotiated the Zomba deal – music and publishing – and the band signed with me,' said Tristram, anxious to get on with it. 'Danny threw a wobbly, refused to sign anything and flounced off somewhere. He went on a bender for weeks, wouldn't take calls or answer the door. In the end we sacked him.'

'Yeah, OK, so what's the biggie here?' said Kris,

'Happens all the time.' He waved a fiver at Alex, 'Get a round in mate, my throat feels like Ozzy's halfway through No Rest for the Wicked' Alex left them and pushed his way to the bar through giggling girls with tinsel and fake snow in their hair and on their clothes. A couple tried to get him under the mistletoe without much luck. The band sat in silence until he returned with a tray of drinks and a plate of mince pies courtesy of the pub landlord.

'Go on, Tristram,' said Alex. He was anxious to get on; it was all beginning to do his head in.

'We got a call about six weeks later from his mate Fizz, the singer with Loved Up, saying that, Danny was, um,' Tristram cleared his throat and waited a moment, taking a deep breath. 'Danny had um, had died.' He rubbed his eyes, shaking his head wearily. 'He'd hanged himself in his mate's recording studio at the back of his house.' Tristram looked up, pain in his eyes. 'He did it with some studio cable on Christmas Eve.'

Buff and Geoff glanced at each other but said nothing. Death was nothing new to them, both having lost many musician friends over the years to drugs and booze.

'What?' Alex screwed his face up. 'What a big girl's blouse!' he laughed, looking around expecting similar reactions from Kris and Gary. They looked stunned. Roy Wood and Wizzard belted out 'I Wish it Could be Christmas Every Day.'

'Can't someone turn that bloody thing off?' shouted Tristram at the juke box. Nobody in the pub took any

150

notice, not that they'd heard; it was Christmas Eve and they were out to celebrate.

So much for sympathy, thought Jonty, for whom the whole episode was doubly raw at this time of year. He'd been mates with Jet and Danny since primary school. He'd always wanted Danny to join the band on bass, not keys, but Danny had always had a reason not to join them. When he finally agreed Jonty and Jet thought he was as committed as they were. They hoped they'd wean him off of keyboards eventually. It was a shock when he got sacked; both musicians believed he'd see sense and come crawling back after a while, but he didn't. He killed himself instead. The guilt nearly destroyed them both and it was months before they could rehearse or record without thinking they could hear him playing his favourite melody on his Fender Rhodes or strumming his Warwick bass. Finding a bass player and drummer had been left to Tristram. They hadn't the heart for it.

'Shut the fuck up, Alex, you cold bastard,' shouted Jet. 'He was our mate, whatever our differences, he was a mate.'

The meat raffle kicked off and it grew a little quieter in the pub as the ticket numbers were called and winners collected their joints of meat and fresh turkeys. In the public bar several meat pie sellers were making their rounds, carrying baskets filled with locally made pasties and pork pies. Cliff Richard blasted out 'Mistletoe and Wine,' and several girls joined in loudly, oblivious to the drama unfolding nearby.

'What's Danny got to do with the racket on the tracks?' Buff asked the obvious, 'Are you saying it's him?' Geoff rolled his eyes. This was one hell of a gig and no shit.

Tristram bent closer to the others, 'It's him, make no mistake.' Geoff laughed and pulled his jacket over his head and waved his arms, making ghoulish sounds.

Buff hit Geoff's shoulder. 'Shut up.' He looked Tristram directly in the eye. 'Spill,' he said. The others shifted in their seats, Jet and Jonty looked utterly miserable but said nothing.

'Danny used to play that melody all the time when messing around on his Fender, he used it to warm up; he never finished writing it. Jet and Jonty recognised it as well. It's him on the tracks.' Tristram took a long slug of beer. He said, 'When he was found in the studio, Slade was belting out – 'Merry Christmas Everybody,' – he hated it.'

'So what's his beef then?' Buff asked. 'Why's he giving it some wellie now?'

'I don't know, but something's upset him,' said Jet. Jonty nodded.

'Listen to yourselves, 'something's upset him,' are you serious?' Gary threw his head back and laughed. 'Guy's fuckin' dead!'

'Ghosts, ghoulies, phantoms and … Danny!' giggled Alex. 'What are you like?'

Roars of laughter and shouting from other customers penetrated Tristram's brain. 'I can't talk here, let's go back to the studio.' He got up, drained his drink, and headed to the exit. Jet and Jonty followed, with Buff and Geoff not far behind.

Kris looked at the others, uncertain. 'You coming?' He really wanted to know what was going on. Gary and Alex nodded, drained their drinks, and left with Kris.

Back in the studio kitchen they sat at the table with coffee and waited. 'I think he's pissed off with how the band's working out,' said Jonty after a while. 'I feel he sees the opportunities we've had and what we could have and I think he's trying to warn you …' He looked at Alex, Kris, and Gary, then Jet and Buff, 'warn *us*, that if we don't stop fighting and falling out, it's all going to be for nothing.'

'Right, some sort of phantom from the grave with a message,' laughed Alex. 'A sort of rock 'n' roll Scrooge and the Ghost of Christmas Past shit.'

'I think Jonty's right,' said Tristram. 'I think Danny screwed up big time and he doesn't want his mates to go the same way.' He really felt Danny was trying to warn them and this was his way.

'We didn't know him, so why should he care?' Gary asked, lighting another smoke.

'He was our mate, he cared about us and I think he doesn't want to see us fall apart and lose it all,' said Jet. 'He can see how it is, and I for one don't want to see another five years of hard work go down the pan.'

'I'll ask him, shall I?' Alex opened the studio door and went inside. Immediately the lights started flickering. 'Hi, Danny, it's me, Alex. Come out, wherever you are.' The others followed him reluctantly. 'See, he's not here.' The lights went out as

Geoff closed the door.

For a moment they stood in darkness and silence, adjusting their eyes. A dim light remained in the vocal booth, spilling shadows over the mixing desk. 'Try the lights, Geoff,' said Buff, sitting in his chair.

'Nope,' Geoff kept trying the main switches but nothing. He went to the back of the desk took a torch from the back shelf, put it on and slide underneath where he fiddled with the cables, reattaching them. 'Try the channels, Buff,' he said, popping his head over the back of the desk. 'Anything?' Buff slid a few faders, changing channels, expecting the guitar tracks to play quietly, but all they could hear was keyboards.

'Yep. It's on all the channels, it's crazy.' Buff turned the volume off. Suddenly the lights flickered and died as the vocal booth filled with a blue tinged mist. It swirled around at shoulder height and as they watched the room grew so cold they could see their own breath. 'Merry Christmas Everybody' filled the studio briefly, so loud they clapped their hands over their ears. It stopped; all they could hear was deep breathing, on the mic. Then, 'Testing, testing, one, two, three.' The voice was unmistakable. Tristram, Jonty, and Jet froze. The others gaped at the shimmering outline of a man standing at the mic.

'Tristram, hey, man; you got what you wanted, but it's not looking great,' the voice said. Tristram grabbed the desk for support, speechless.

'Jonty, Jet, my old mates. Stabbed me in the back, but that's cool; would've done the same.' The two musicians held their breath. 'I forgive you, it's in the

154

past.'

'Wha ... why?' Tristram stuttered. 'Danny, it can't be ...'

'Yep. It is.' Danny laughed a soulless laugh. 'Been watching you; gotta say, mate, you guys suck.' Danny's ghostly form gradually looked more solid, more human, as he spoke.

'You know, at first I wanted to take it all away from you guys,' Danny's voice shook, 'You didn't deserve having what I lost, but you know what?' Danny's breath filled the mic. 'I like the new music, I think it's got legs.' He sighed. 'I'd never have made it, I know that now. You guys wanted it real bad. I just wanted the glamour, the fame, and the lifestyle. It'd never have worked ... I know now; it's all about the music.'

'Danny, why? Why did you do it?' Jonty was almost crying. 'I've had nightmares. Jet nearly lost it ... why?'

'Man, you'll love this,' Danny giggled. 'It was a mistake, an accident. Remember that chick from A&M, the one looked like butter wouldn't melt?' Both musicians and their manager nodded.

'Well, me and her we sort of got into it, in the studio, and her old man came barging in just at the wrong moment.' Danny coughed long and hard. 'Thing is, he didn't see the cable round my neck and he shoved me hard. I fell off the chair.' Danny paused 'Bingo!'

'But if someone was there, why didn't they help you?' Jet couldn't believe it. 'Surely she tried, even if her old man didn't?'

'Too late, mate. I was so high I vomited and choked on it and by the time they realised, it was, like, well, they wanted out of there.' Danny sighed. 'They came back later, dressed me and put me back so it looked like I'd kicked the chair away; done deal, no-one checked. Just another drugged-up sex game gone wrong. No-one wanted a scandal so they managed to cover it all up – even Tristram worked his magic.

'God, Danny, mate, that's tragic.' Jonty had tears streaming down his face. 'No-one breathed a word. We just heard you'd hanged yourself, nothing was mentioned about what you just said …' Jonty shook his head. 'We've been so cut up, especially at Christmas, because, well, you know … the date.'

'Look, you three.' He gestured to Twister's newest members. 'Don't throw it all away being shits. It doesn't last and stuff gets in the way of the music.' His hands shimmered as he moved them. 'I had it and lost it and regret being such a shit, but you guys, you've got it all – and the way you're going on, well, you're gonna blow it.'

Kris, Gary, and Alex stared, unable to speak. 'Don't be dumb, you're making enemies, losing friends, and soon the fans will get fed up with the nasty rep you all have.' Danny's voice was weak and regretful. 'Buff is a cool guy, he doesn't deserve this crap; Geoff doesn't deserve it. Think, will ya?'

Danny's image shimmied and began to fade. 'Don't forget. Don't screw it up, guys. Make it for me, your old mate is watching.' His presence drifted away, 'I love you guys.' Then he was gone. The lights came

156

back on and the desk lit up. The room was warmer.

'We didn't get to ask anything,' Gary said. 'I don't believe it.'

Tristram cleared his throat. 'OK guys, you heard what Danny said, I was going to have this chat with you anyway, but we'll have it now.' He looked around the room. 'Are you going to change your attitude, your behaviour, grow up and work hard, or are you going to throw it all away? Choice is yours. I for one haven't the time or money to waste.'

The members of Twister looked back at him, at Buff and Geoff, and each nodded sincerely. 'I think we all agree, Tristram, we're going to change and things are going to be different. Better. Right, guys?' Gary said.

'We apologise, Buff, Geoff. We won't be such shits to work with from now on,' said Alex, and Gary gave the thumbs-up.

'Cool,' said Kris. 'It's been so stressful. You know I have to watch my stress levels.' Everyone laughed. Who didn't know about his stress levels?

'OK guys we'll do it,' Buff said and Geoff smiled back 'Yep.'

'A new start for a new year and we'll do Danny proud,' said Jonty, gazing at the vocal booth.

'Love you, Danny boy, this is for you,' said Jet, a lump in his throat.

'Merry Christmas Everybody,' screeched from the monitors followed by a long hearty laugh. 'I'll be watching you guys.' Danny's voice filled the studio as Slade boomed from the monitors. This time no-one was angry or frightened. They all sang along and for once the studio was filled with laughter and happiness and hope.

'Right, guys, back to work. We have an album to make and A&R will be here next week,' said Tristram. 'I think the tracks will be keyboard-free from now on.'

Buff rode the faders and set up the track ready for Alex to do his vocal, alone this time. 'Alex, come on, let's do it.'

'OK, Buff, I'm on it.' Alex went into the booth and put his cans on. 'I'm watching you, Alex.' Danny's voice filled the cans. 'Don't forget.'

'I won't,' said Alex.

'What's that?' ssked Buff.

'Nothing, Buff, just thinking time's money.' Alex laughed and then sang at the top of his voice, 'Merry Christmas!'

Danny's voice filled the monitors as he sang the chorus with him and Twister joined in.

'The things I do to pay for my ex-wife,' muttered Buff. Geoff silently thanked the stars above that he was single.

Family Matters

Jane Jackson

'Rob, that's unfair.' Jess's grip on the phone tightened. Realising her knuckles were aching she swapped the phone to her other ear and flexed her fingers. 'I'd love to have Helen for the day. I just can't manage this week because –' There was a click. 'I have commitments too,' she finished to the sound of the dialling tone.

Anger flared but quickly faded as she replaced the receiver. He sounded stressed and exhausted. Drunks, car smashes, overdoses, fights, and broken bones: the demands on A&E would be non-stop and it was still a week until Christmas Eve.

But her accounting work wasn't a hobby. Nor were the family trees she compiled. They were paying jobs. She needed the money and had given her word. Though she understood the reason for Rob's short temper, being on the receiving end of it wasn't pleasant.

Hearing Tom's familiar knock lifted her mood. She hurried to open the door.

'Come in.' She stood back, happy to see him. Springy fair hair now threaded with silver had been tamed with water and a comb. His dark brown waxed jacket was unzipped revealing a navy crew-neck sweater over a checked shirt and clean jeans. 'You look smart.'

'I can scrub up when I need to.' He grinned, his teeth white against his weathered tan. He leaned in to kiss her cheek. 'Hello, my bird.' His lips were soft and warm and he smelled of soap and fresh air. He straightened. 'Don't mind do you?'

'A kiss? No, I don't mind. It was nice.'

'I don't want to mess up this time.'

'You didn't mess up. We were young and wanted different things.' Jess touched his face lightly then crossed the open-plan living room to the kitchen area. 'We'd better get going. The concert starts at seven thirty and it's almost ten to. It'll be a push to get all the food plated up and the crockery set out before the singing starts. Will you bring those?'

He lifted the two shopping bags filled with plastic containers off the worktop.

'Dear life, Jess. How many are you feeding?'

'That won't go far. There are thirty in the choir – thirty-three if you include Margaret the accompanist, conductor Dennis, and our soloist Morwenna. They all eat like gannets after a concert. At least half the village will stay for a cup of tea and a chat. But Viv has promised sandwiches. Morwenna said she'd pick up three dozen splits, and Gill is bringing sausage rolls and a fruitcake. Knowing her she'll have persuaded some of the WI to donate quiches and tray-bakes.'

'Good job the rain's stopped,' Tom said. 'People don't like coming out in the wet. How many tickets have sold?'

'All of them. Because it's for charity Gill wouldn't have let anyone leave the post office without buying one even if they can't come.'

As Jess went to fetch her pink padded jacket from the hook behind the door, Tom dropped the bags and got there first, holding it so she could push her arms into the sleeves. She felt his hands rest briefly on her shoulders.

Scarred, callused, *gentle* hands. A man she could trust. But was she ready? Was it too soon? Returning to the village where she had grown up had helped her move on from the shock of Alex's death and the shattering discovery that he had left her with a re-mortgaged house and no money. She had known Tom since they were children. He'd been her first love. But they had spent nearly three decades apart and people changed. She had. There'd been no choice.

Zipping up her jacket she pulled a pink knitted hat over her cropped curls, picked up the basket holding a deep round cake tin, two jars of jam, and a large tub of cream. As Tom stepped outside she switched off the light.

'How did it go today?'

'I'll tell you later.'

'I wasn't asking out of politeness.' She locked the door.

'I know, bird. But it'll take a while and there isn't time now.'

Jess led the way down the narrow garden path to the road. 'Will you take *Mary-Louise* out tomorrow?' she asked over her shoulder.

'Depends on the forecast. I'll need to drive her hard to test the new rig. But I'm not risking it if there's a gale blowing. The owner is coming down next week. I want him happy so I can get paid.' He hesitated. 'Like to come out with me would you?'

'Sailing?' The streetlight outside the village shop

162

was off again. The air was cold and clear and against the inky sky stars twinkled like scattered diamonds. One was very bright. 'Tom, it's the middle of December.' She shivered.

'Put an extra vest on. Come on, girl. It would do you good to have a few hours away from figures and research.'

Briefly tempted Jess remembered Rob's phone call. 'I can't. I've got an accounting job and a family tree to finish before Christmas. Ask me again in April.'

'It'll go in my new diary, in red,' he promised.

He stepped in front of her forcing her to stop then leaned down and kissed her cheek again. 'How did I ever let you go?'

'Hey, no kissing in the street.'

His teeth flashed as he grinned. 'How about later?'

'Don't push it.'

'Got to. I don't want anyone else snapping you up.'

'Tom, I'm forty-eight and a grandmother. There won't be a queue.'

'Go on, lovely you are.'

'Stop it! If Gill or Viv hear you they'll be choosing flowers and planning the reception. I know it's been two years. But sometimes it feels like it all happened yesterday.'

'Sorry, bird. I don't mean no harm.'

She smiled at him. 'I know. And your interest is very flattering –'

'Flattery be bug – blowed,' he corrected hastily as they crossed the yard to the village hall's back door. 'I meant every word. I want another chance, Jess. But I

163

can wait.' He pushed a key into the lock.

She nudged him. 'You always say the right thing.'

'I'm working on it.' He bumped her arm gently. 'And you.' Inserting the key he turned it both ways. 'I don't know why we bother with a lock.'

Jess stepped inside and pressed the switch on the wall at the bottom of a narrow staircase with bare wooden treads. 'Harry will have been in to switch on the heating. I bet he forgot to lock up again when he went over to the pub.'

Two neon strips flickered and filled the kitchen with bright light. To the left of the kitchen door a narrow wooden staircase led up to a tiny landing and a storage room.

Jess set her basket on the worktop that ran round two walls with cupboards below. A sink with double-draining board stood beneath the window. Between the kitchen and the main body of the hall a wide serving hatch with closed folding doors was set into the wall above the work surface.

'Give me a minute to fill the urn and I'll give you a hand to carry down the screens and the lectern.'

'They're too heavy –'

'Not with two of us.'

As Tom started up to the storeroom Jess opened a cupboard, took out a large plastic jug, and held it under the tap. Tipping the water into the urn she refilled the jug.

Tom stopped on the staircase. 'Jess!' he hissed. 'Did you hear that?'

'Hear what?' She turned off the tap.

'Someone's up there.' He pointed to the ceiling, his voice low.

'How do you know?'

'I heard a girl moaning and a bloke trying to quiet her.'

Jess stared at him trying not to laugh at his obvious discomfort. 'Do you think they're …?'

'How should I know?' Their eyes met.

'Well, whoever it is they shouldn't be up there,' Jess had lowered her voice to match Tom's. Tipping the second full jug into the urn, she flicked the switch on the wall and refilled the jug once more. 'Up you go then.' She nodded towards the stairs. 'Margaret needs the screens and Dennis needs the lectern. Stamp your feet and cough loudly. That should give them time to make themselves decent.'

He gripped the worn banister, visibly reluctant. 'Why me?'

'You're a man, you heard them first, and you're already on the stairs.'

'God, you're a hard woman.'

Her smile was wry. 'I wish.'

At the sound of another muffled moan he grinned. 'Remember the old boatshed?'

'I remember the smell. Musty canvas, old rope, varnish, seaweed, and mud.'

'Happy days though.'

'Another life. Tom, you have to get them out.'

Clearing his throat loudly he thumped up the wooden treads turning to glare over his shoulder as she snorted, trying to smother a giggle. On the small landing at the top he hesitated then rapped on the wooden door.

'Come on. Time to go. You shouldn't even be here.'

Jess heard him open the door. There was a pause. 'What –?' He broke off as a man's voice pleaded.

Curious, Jess crossed to the staircase still holding the knife she was using to slice the cinnamon-flavoured fruit loaf she had baked the previous day. She saw Tom back out, one hand raised.

'Stay … Don't … I'll …' Pulling the door closed he bolted down, stopping when he saw her. 'Jess, you need to get up here.'

'They need to leave. Gill and the others will be arriving any minute.'

'They aren't going anywhere. Not without an ambulance. She's pregnant. I think the baby's coming.'

'Now?' Dropping her knife onto the worktop Jess raced up the stairs. At the top he opened the door and stood back to let her pass.

Near the far wall, in a cleared space among the stacked hard-backed chairs, tables, and two decorated Chinese screens, a young Asian man was kneeling beside an old sofa. He was unshaven. Black hair curled on his wet shirt collar. The lower legs of his trousers and his shoes were soaked. Two coats tossed over a wooden chair dripped onto the bare boards beside two sodden rucksacks. He looked up, his face haggard with exhaustion and anxiety.

'Please help us. Farah – the baby – it's not due for

166

three weeks.'

Jess looked from him to the sofa where an olive-skinned, dark-haired girl swathed in a thick grey cardigan over a rust-brown tunic and trousers lay on her side, clutching the young man's hand. There were dark shadows beneath her closed eyes as she panted for breath. She looked very young and very tired.

The girl's face tightened and she moaned. As she turned on the sofa Jess saw her swollen belly. She turned to the young man. 'I'm Jess. This is Tom.' She crouched beside the girl. 'Farah? Do you think your baby's coming?' The girl nodded.

'What's your name?' Tom asked the young man who hesitated. 'We'll help, but we need to know what to call you.'

'Khalid. I am Malik Khalid Khan.'

'Where are you from?'

'Birmingham.' He must have seen the shock in their exchanged glance. 'We're not illegal, we were born in Britain. So were our parents. But they still follow the old traditions.'

'Khalid,' Jess said, 'Farah should be in hospital. Tom, there's no mobile signal here. Go back to my place and phone for an ambulance –'

'No!' the young man shot to his feet.

'Steady,' Tom warned. 'Calm down.'

'You don't understand. If Farah goes to hospital there'll be records, paperwork. No one must know where we are.'

'She's in labour,' Jess said. 'She needs medical attention.'

'You think I don't know that?' Khalid's tone was anguished. 'But the risk's too great.'

'What risk? What are you talking about?

'If they find us they'll kill us.'

'Who will?'

'Farah's father and brothers. That's why we're trying to get to France.'

'*Kill* you? Come on. Why would they do that?'

The young man straightened up. 'You think I'm making this up? Don't you read the papers? Haven't you seen the reports about honour killings on TV? For each one on the news there are many more that are hushed up and never investigated.' He rubbed his face as if to banish the fatigue and strain etched on it.

'Farah and I met at college and we became close. Her family didn't know. They wouldn't have permitted –' He stopped, took a breath. 'They arranged her marriage to a man they'd chosen. Her refusal to accept it dishonoured both families. Friends helped us escape to London. We found work and a place to live. We thought we were safe. But someone betrayed us. Her family will not forgive or forget. If we're found … Please. No hospital.'

Jess heard the back door open. Tom peered down then came back in. 'Gill and Morwenna.'

Khalid gripped Jess's arm. 'You can't –'

She covered his hand with her own. 'I have to. There's a concert tonight in the hall. Those ladies have come to help prepare refreshments. They're bound to guess something's going on.'

With a reluctant nod he knelt by the sofa and

smoothed wet strands of hair off Farah's forehead. She bit back a groan.

Jess turned to Tom. 'I'll tell Gill and ask her to fetch Annie Rogers. Annie was a midwife,' she explained to Khalid.

'She's been retired twenty years,' Tom whispered in Jess's ear.

'Giving birth hasn't changed and she's delivered scores of babies. Besides, if we can't call the paramedics we need her. Let's get the lectern down. You can come back for the screens while I tell Gill and Morwenna.'

Before he could reply, Farah compressed her lips, her face contorting as she writhed on the sofa.

Glancing back, Jess saw Khalid kiss her hand then press it to his chest as he stroked her face, murmuring reassurance.

'Bloody hell,' Tom muttered.

'You said it.' As they carried the lectern carefully down the narrow staircase, Jess heard the strain in Morwenna's voice.

'Mother wanted me to stay home.' She removed a plastic rain hat from her frizzy perm, hung up her coat on one of the pegs near the door, then tugged her black cardigan down over plump hips swathed in a long black skirt. Beneath the cardigan she wore a silky white blouse that emphasised her high colour. 'She've known for weeks that I'm singing solos tonight. I told her she didn't need to come but I had to.'

Catching Jess's eye Tom shook his head. 'Has Brenda Crocker ever seen a happy day?'

169

'Hello, Morwenna,' Jess called over Tom's head. 'Did you bring the splits?'

'On the worktop,' Morwenna pointed. 'Start slicing and spreading shall I? My stomach's in uproar. I'll be better if I'm doing something.'

'First will you fill the kettle and boil it?' At the bottom of the stairs they put the lectern down. Tom ran back up and moments later walked one black-painted folding screen onto the small landing. After fetching the second he quickly closed the door. While he carried each one down, propping them against the banister at the bottom, Jess crossed to the postmistress. Still wearing her heather tweed coat, Gill unloaded four two-litre bottles milk from one basket. From the other she was lifting out cake tins.

'Harry's out the front unlocking the doors. Reeking of whisky he is. I thought the rain might put people off. But they're coming early to get the best seats. The village do dearly love a carol concert.' She glanced sideways at Jess.

'All right, bird?' Her smile faded to a frown. 'What's wrong?'

Laying a hand on Gill's arm, Jess called over her shoulder. 'Morwenna? Can you come here a minute?'

Morwenna put down the tea caddy and joined them. Keeping an eye on the back door that led outside to the covered way and the stage door Jess spoke quickly. 'There's a young couple upstairs in the props room. They aren't local. The girl is pregnant and the baby is coming.'

Morwenna's bushy eyebrows shot up. 'What,

now?'

Jess nodded. 'I think so. But she can't go to hospital.'

'Why not?'

'Because they're hiding from people who would hurt them.'

'Haven't they got family?'

'It's their families they're running away from. Gill, we need Annie. Could you –?'

'On my way.' Pulling a scarf from her pocket, Gill tied it over her freshly set hair as she hurried to the door.

'Morwenna, will you make a pot of tea?' Jess blew out a breath and turned to the worktop. A muffled groan made them both look up.

'What if people hear?' Morwenna whispered, lifting the brown teapot of a shelf beside the sink.

'We'll have to make sure they don't.' Jess started transferring mince pies from a plastic container to a large blue china plate. 'If people have started arriving there'll soon be plenty of noise and chatter in the hall. Once the concert begins we need you to give it all you've got and encourage the audience to join in the choruses.'

Panic crossed Morwenna's face. 'But there aren't no song-sheets.'

'It's a carol concert, Mor,' Jess reminded her with a smile. 'People know most of the words by heart.'

''Course they do.' She clicked her tongue. 'Don't mind me. 'Tis just – what with Mother and now this –'

'The choir will carry them through any verses they

aren't sure of.' Jess opened a jar of homemade strawberry jam and began spreading it onto the sliced splits.

Downy as a peach, Morwenna's round face was flushed with excitement and unease as she unscrewed the top on a plastic bottle of milk and peeled off the silver foil. 'Sing my heart out, I will. But you know what the village is like. Nothing stays secret for long.'

'It certainly doesn't,' Jess murmured.

'I never asked, Jess. Not even when Mother told me to.'

Jess's smile was wry. 'I knew there'd be gossip. During my marriage I lived in a big house in Truro. After my husband died I moved back here to a small cottage. People were bound to wonder where the money had gone.'

Morwenna shook her head. 'Tom don't care about that.'

'Tom is … we're friends, that's all.'

'I should think so too. You've knowed each other since you was children. Now he's divorced and you're a widow –'

'Morwenna!'

'Well, you was close once. We all thought you'd get married.'

'But we didn't. Anyway right now there are more important things to think about. We have to keep this secret until the baby's born and the family can be moved somewhere safe.'

'After they're gone I can tell Mother?'

Jess nodded.

'She'll be spitting feathers that she didn't come tonight.' Morwenna's brief gleeful smile gave way to anxiety. 'I'd better make that tea. Be glad of a cup myself. I never had time for one at home.' She warmed the pot, made the tea, then refilled the kettle and switched it on. 'Not after making Mother's, then getting her washed and changed and finding her programme on the TV.'

'I'll fix you a plate.' Jess spooned clotted cream from a tub onto the jam-topped splits. 'You'll need your strength tonight, and so will we.'

Opening a cupboard beneath the wide worktop above the serving hatch, Morwenna lifted out short stacks of saucers followed by every cup she could find. They rattled in her unsteady hands. 'We'll never have enough. Gill said the concert is sold out. There's all the choir and –'

'We'll have plenty,' Jess reassured. 'Not everyone will stay on afterwards. We'll ask those who are first in the queue to bring their cups back to the hatch when they've finished so they can be washed up ready for those who come up later.'

Tom came back and picked up the second screen. 'Hall's starting to fill. Want me to come back when I've set these up for Margaret?'

'You're a gem.'

'Hold that thought.'

Opening the second of Gill's plastic containers, Jess lifted out a sausage roll and put it on a small plate, added a split topped with jam and cream, and handed them to Morwenna.

'Pull out one of those stools and sit for a minute while you eat this. I'll pour the tea.'

As she was speaking, Gill came in through the back door carrying two plastic bags.

'What's all that? Jess asked.

'Towels, bin bags, newspapers, and an old sheet,' Annie Rogers said following Gill inside.

'Evening, Jess. Morwenna, you're looking some smart.' Annie dropped a large scuffed black leather bag and shrugged off her raincoat to reveal a pair of black stretch trousers covered with snags and cat hairs, topped by a baggy red jumper over a red tartan shirt. Her grey hair was twisted up into a cottage-loaf bun on top of her head, a hairstyle she hadn't altered in forty years.

'Thanks for coming, Annie.' Jess passed the coat to Gill who hung hers and Annie's in the corner cupboard out of sight.

'I went to the nativity play up at the school this afternoon, that's how I wasn't coming tonight. Is it right what Gill said? This couple is running from family?'

Jess nodded. 'They were born in this country but their background is Asian and their parents are traditional. Farah refused an arranged marriage. She and Khalid were trying to leave the country because they're afraid her father and brothers will kill her for dishonouring the family.'

Annie gave a snort of disgust. 'Don't see much honour in murdering your own daughter. Right, I need a basin, hot and cold water, and a bucket.'

174

'D'you want an apron? Jess reached towards a drawer.

'Brought my own.' Lifting the bags, Annie started up the stairs. 'That kettle boiled? Bring it up along with the rest, soon as you can.'

Another muffled moan sent Jess across the kitchen. From the cupboard under the sink she fetched a bucket. In it she placed the largest plastic bowl she could find.

Morwenna poured three cups of tea, bit into a sausage roll, and continued spreading jam on the rest of the splits.

Gill glanced up from arranging slices of quiche on more blue plates. 'If her labour's started – Farah is it? Pretty name. She won't want anything. But the lad might be glad of a hot drink and a bite to eat.'

Jess could have kicked herself. 'I never thought –'

'Dear life, girl, you can't think of everything. You take those things to Annie. I'll set a tray.' She turned as Tom came in through the hall door. 'Tom, if you've got the keys, lock both doors. But let Viv in when she comes. Anyone who's brought food can pass it through the hatch.'

With a nod and a brief glance at Jess that made her feel warm inside, Tom went out through the back door.

There he was, doing what was asked without arguing or needing to take charge. She knew from observation and experience that was rare in a man. Filling a tall enamel jug with cold water she hurried upstairs.

Khalid had pulled out an upright chair and was

sitting by Farah's head with his back to Annie, who had a stethoscope pressed to the taut mound of Farah's belly.

Setting down bucket, basin, and jug within Annie's reach, Jess straightened up. 'Is there anything else you need?'

Annie removed the earpieces and hooked them around her neck. 'Another large basin and some supper for young mister here.'

'Gill's getting a tray ready.'

Khalid looked round, features tight, eyes narrowed in anger that couldn't hide his fear. 'How can I eat?'

'You'll be no good to your girl if you don't,' Annie said. 'She needs you to be strong. So does this baby. You got trouble enough. Don't go looking for more.' She paused, her abrupt manner softening a fraction. 'Come on, my 'andsome, a blind man could see you're hungry.'

Annie's flat gaze held Khalid's stormy one. He broke first and turned his head.

'What about baby clothes?' Jess asked. 'Khalid?'

'There are a few things in Farah's rucksack. We had much more but –' His eyes filling, he swallowed hard.

'Never mind,' Jess said. 'I bought a couple of sleep suits and vests for my little granddaughter. As soon as the concert starts I'll run home and fetch them.' Waving away his thanks, she crossed to the door.

'Jess,' Annie stopped her. 'I'll need a pack of pads, large size, and disposable nappies.'

As a groan was forced from Farah's lips, Jess

glanced at her watch. 7.25. She hoped the concert started on time.

In the kitchen Gill had folded back one of the hatch doors. Leaning forward she shouted, 'Anyone who has brought refreshments bring them here to me.'

Several women hurried over with tins and Tupperware but didn't linger, anxious to return to their seats.

The back door opened admitting Tom and the sound of male voices laughing and bantering.

'The choir's going in through the stage door,' he said searching the bunch of keys.

'Hang on, Tom,' Gill said. 'Don't lock our soloist in. We need her out there tonight.'

Draining her cup, Morwenna wiped her mouth with a hanky that she tucked up her sleeve. Unbuttoning her cardigan she pulled it off.

'Give it to me,' Gill said. 'I'll put it with our coats. Now you go out there and lift the roof off.'

'Here,' Jess held out a half-full glass of water. 'Leave it in the wings. If it's there you won't need it.'

Settling the lapels of her cream blouse Morwenna took a deep breath and lifted her chin. Beaming at Jess and Gill she took the glass. 'We'll give that baby a proper welcome.'

Viv arrived as Morwenna was leaving. 'All right, Mor? How's your mother?'

'Same as usual.'

Viv nodded in sympathy. 'Sorry I'm late,' she said as Tom relocked the kitchen door. 'Jimmy was late home then the cat was sick.' Short and barrel-shaped,

Viv placed a large square biscuit tin on the stairs and shrugged off a gold anorak with a fur-lined hood, revealing purple leggings and a tomato red sweatshirt.

Gill blinked. 'Dear life, Viv. Where's my dark glasses? Stop traffic, you would.'

'Go on, you're just jealous.' Viv picked up the tin and brought it to the worktop. 'I like red. It cheers me up.'

'We could do with some of that tonight,' Tom said, climbing the stairs ahead of Jess who was carrying the tray Gill had prepared.

'Why? What's –'

'You tell her, Gill,' Jess said over her shoulder.

As well as two plates of food, one savoury one sweet, and a cup of tea for Khalid, the tray also held one for Annie and a glass of cold water and a spoon so Khalid could feed Farah sips.

Tom opened the door, pulling it closed again as soon as Jess had stepped inside. Khalid jumped to his feet and lifted another hard wooden chair from the pile, clearly relieved to have something to do. Jess placed the tray on it then carried one cup and the glass of water to Annie who was spreading an old towel over a wad of open newspapers on a black bin bag.

'Thanks, Jess. Put them back out of the way so I don't knock them over.' She smiled at Farah. 'Roll over a minute, my bird, so I can slide this underneath you. And back again. There, that's handsome.' She covered Farah with the blanket.

Jess crouched by Khalid, who had turned his chair so he could not see Farah's body or Annie. She felt for

178

him. Not every man would choose to attend the birth of his child. Not every woman wanted her husband or partner present.

'Why don't you go and sit over there while you eat.' She nodded towards a space behind the door. 'Farah couldn't be better looked after. Annie has delivered hundreds of babies.'

'I should not be here, seeing this,' he whispered.

'Would you like to go downstairs with Gill, Viv, and Tom? The doors are locked. No one else can come in.'

'No, I can't leave her. But watching her suffer –'

'Come on,' Jess slipped her hand under his arm, guided him across to the space behind the door and, pulling a chair around pushed him onto it.

Through two closed doors she heard a burst of applause. Margaret Hitchens played the introductory bars to 'Silent Night'. Hearing Morwenna's clear soprano, recalling the excitement on her face as she promised to sing her heart out, Jess felt a thickness in her throat.

Though the past two years had seen her life change out of all recognition, she had so much to be grateful for.

Her gaze fell on a pile of folded materials of different colours and textures. Alongside were coils of frayed rope removed when those drawing the heavy stage curtains were replaced and kept in case one day they might be of use.

'Annie, how about I rig up a curtain to give you and Farah some privacy?'

Annie's gaze flicked towards Khalid who was sitting bent forward, elbows on his thighs, head in his hands. She gave a brief nod. Raising her voice she spoke to Khalid. 'That food won't eat itself, boy. I want to see those plates clean. I can't be doing with you passing out.'

He jerked upright. 'I won't. I –'

'You'll eat the supper these ladies have been good enough to prepare for you. All right?'

'Yes, Miss – er … Mrs –'

'Annie will do just fine. Well? What are you waiting for?'

Catching her lower lip between her teeth to hold back a grin, Jess tied one end of the rope to a curved wrought iron coat hook, the innermost of six mounted on a painted board nailed to the wall alongside the window. Annie had all the finesse of a steamroller. But beneath her blunt manner her heart was marshmallow.

Crossing the room, Jess looped the rope around an old gas mantle bracket fixed to the inner wall. Pulling it tight and tying it off, she let the remaining rope hang down the wall and pool on the floor. Unfolding one of the curtains with care to avoid releasing too much dust she hung it over the taut line. Now Farah, Annie, and the sofa were hidden from anyone entering the room. Jess turned to reach for a second curtain but Khalid, hastily swallowing a mouthful of cheese and onion quiche, had already picked it up.

Behind the curtain Farah groaned, her voice rising.

'Why are you being so kind?' he whispered as they hung faded crimson velvet over the rope and pulled it straight.

'You needed help.'

'You don't know us.'

'What's that got to do with anything? I have children, so do Tom and Viv. Gill lost a son to meningitis. Before Annie retired she delivered many of the children born in this village. Most of them are down in the hall with their families singing carols to celebrate the birth of Jesus. In an hour or two you and Farah won't be a couple, you'll be a family. You can make your own traditions.' She patted his arm and grinned. 'This may not be where you'd have chosen for your baby to be born. But it's better than a stable.'

She drew him back to his chair. 'Sit down. Finish your supper. If you don't mind me asking, why did you come to Cornwall?'

'We didn't plan to. We caught a train to Plymouth for the Roscoff ferry where friends would meet us.'

'What went wrong?'

Khalid raked his hair. 'I had checked the timetable so I knew that in December there are no sailings at the beginning of the week. We intended to catch the Thursday evening one. But the booking clerk told us that it had been cancelled because of a strike at Roscoff. We went to the cafeteria to decide what to do. Farah wasn't feeling well.'

'I'm not surprised, poor girl.'

'She's had contractions before, especially this past month. There's a name –' he broke off, frowning as he tried to remember.

'Braxton Hicks?'

Khalid nodded. 'We hoped her pains were just stress. Then a lorry driver came over. He'd heard us talking to the booking clerk. He told us he lived in Cornwall and was on his way home. He said if we were willing to pay he knew someone with a boat who would take us over to France.'

About to speak, Jess bit her tongue instead. Khalid nodded.

'I know. Why would we trust him? But I was desperate. He dropped us off by the pub car park. He said to wait under the trees and someone would come. He said the boatman would need to buy fuel to take us across. I gave him £40 and said we'd pay the rest once we reached France. We waited and waited. It was raining and Farah's pains were coming more often. I didn't want to go into the pub, in a small place people remember strangers, but we needed shelter. Then I saw a man go into the hall and lights came on. He'd left the back door open and I could hear him clattering about at the far end. So we came up here. Then the lights went off and he left.'

'Lucky for you the carol concert was tonight,' Jess said.

He shuddered. 'I never should have – but I was so afraid – Farah is everything to me. If anything happens –'

'You're safe. No one knows where you are.'

'The lorry driver –'

'Forget him.' He'll have forgotten you. She kept the thought to herself. 'Would you like anything more to eat?'

182

He shook his head. 'Maybe later.'

'Once this baby arrives Farah will be ravenous. I know I was. I'll put a couple of plates aside.' She put her head round the curtain as Farah sobbed in a breath and opened her eyes.

'Getting stronger are they, bird?' Annie glanced up from tearing the sheet into four pieces. 'Like a drop of water?'

Farah nodded, the tip of her tongue snaking out to moisten her lips.

'Would you, Jess? Not too much.'

Jess held the glass to the girl's lips while she took a mouthful.

'It hurts,' Farah whispered.

'Once your baby's here you'll forget all about this.' Annie unhooked the stethoscope from her neck and gently fitted the earpieces in Farah's ears then held the round end to the girl's belly. 'Hear that? It's your baby's heart beating.'

Wonder softened the girl's strained features. 'Oh!' she breathed. 'It's so fast, like a bird fluttering.' Then she caught her breath, her eyes closing as another contraction took hold.

Gently Annie removed the stethoscope and put it aside. 'Time to get you ready.' She washed and dried her hands, tipped the used water into the bucket, then rinsed and refilled the basin. Handing both kettle and jug to Jess she snapped on a pair of latex gloves.

'Back in a minute.' Jess flashed Khalid a quick smile then closed the door and ran downstairs.

'How's it going?' Tom looked round from plating

sandwiches.

'OK I think. I'd forgotten what hard work childbirth is, though.'

'Good job too,' Viv said. 'If you remembered the pain, you'd never have more than one.'

'Annie bullied Khalid into eating something,' Jess said, busy at the sink. 'Gill, have you got the shop key in your bag?'

'Annie need something, does she?'

'Disposable nappies and pads for Farah.'

Gill grabbed her coat and Tom handed Viv the backdoor key.

'Let her out, Viv.' Tom put his arms around Jess. 'Catch your breath a minute.'

About to push him away, she let her head drop onto his shoulder.

'Doing a grand job, you are,' he murmured. His breath was warm on her neck.

'What'll happen to them, Tom? They can't stay here.'

'I've been thinking about that. Tell you later,' he said as she lifted her head. He planted a kiss on her cheek.

'Here, put her down,' Viv said. 'You haven't finished plating up they sandwiches yet.'

'I'm some proud of you,' he murmured in Jess's ear. 'Go on. You don't want to keep Annie waiting.'

Back upstairs Jess put down the kettle and jug and helped raise Farah while Annie removed the wet pad of towel-covered newspapers, replacing it with another covered with a large square of clean sheet.

'I'll run home and fetch those baby clothes. I won't be long.'

'Don't rush,' Annie warned. 'It's black as your father's hat out there. I don't want you tripping over. I got enough to do.'

Downstairs Jess grabbed her jacket.

'I'll come with you,' Tom said.

'There's no need, I'll only be –'

'I'll come with you,' Tom repeated. He handed the keys to Viv. 'Gill should be back any minute.'

The night air was cold and Jess smelled wood smoke then the scents of beer and frying onions as they hurried past the pub.

Tom waited inside the front door as she grabbed a plastic bag from the cupboard and ran upstairs to the spare bedroom. From the top drawer of the chest she took two tiny white sleep suits and vests, then picked out a couple of towels from the airing cupboard, stuffing them into the bag as she hurried down.

As they crossed the yard Jess heard Morwenna sing the first two lines of 'Ding Dong Merrily on High,' then the choir and the rest of the village joined in the chorus.

Back inside, the door relocked, Jess handed her coat to Tom as Gill came downstairs carrying the kettle and jug.

'Tom, go and talk to that boy. He's fretting and Annie have got her hands full.'

'Me?'

'You're a father,' Jess reminded him. 'You've been through this. Khalid is in strange place among people he doesn't know. He's probably blaming himself for everything that's gone wrong.'

'I can't go in there,' he blurted. 'Not while she's – it's private.'

'You can't see anything –' Gill began.

'I rigged up a curtain,' Jess explained. 'It's no different to being on a hospital ward.'

'Not much it isn't.' But he followed her up. Jess opened the door. Indicating the faded velvet, she bit back a grin at the relief on his face.

As Khalid looked up, Tom picked up two chairs and carried them out onto the small landing.

'Come on, we'll leave the women to it. They know what they're doing. Your girl is in safe hands.'

'I can't –'

'Listen, it'll be harder for her if she's afraid to make a sound in case you panic. But you're here ready to go in when it's time. Had something to eat, have you?'

As the door closed Jess felt herself soften inside. When it came to steamrollers there was little to choose between Tom and Annie.

'It's me, Annie. I've brought the baby clothes and a couple more towels.'

'Come in, Jess. Here, sit and talk to Farah for a minute.

Jess sat on the small hard chair close to Farah's head, facing her. 'Would you like a drop of water?'

Farah moved her head on the cushion Annie had covered with a torn piece of clean sheet. 'Khalid?' she asked in a raspy voice.

'He's out on the landing. Tom is keeping him

company. Can you hear the singing?' The choir had moved on to 'Once in Royal David's City'. Farah nodded. 'Then you can imagine how loud it is down in the hall.'

'No one will hear me?'

Jess shook her head. 'No.'

Farah relaxed. Then her face crumpled as another contraction began. Jess grabbed her hand. 'Don't try to hold it in. Breathe as if you've been running. Like this.' Jess panted. As the contraction progressed, Farah's grip tightened. 'Come on,' Jess urged. 'I learned to do it when I had my twins. I promise it will help.' With Farah's liquid brown eyes fixed on hers, they panted.

The contraction subsided and Jess took a deep breath. Farah did the same. But as her mouth curved in a tired smile, tears slid from the outer corners of her eyes and soaked into the sheet.

Jess's throat ached in sympathy. She'd been alone when the twins were born. Alex had been abroad and her gran too ill to come to the hospital. Though Farah was giving birth among strangers, Khalid was feet away. That he loved her was obvious, and he was suffering on her behalf.

'You're doing brilliantly,' Jess encouraged. 'Isn't she, Annie?'

'Proper job,' Annie said, setting out scissors and other items on a small tray then tearing open a white paper packet.

'That's a yes,' Jess whispered, smoothing sweat-damp hair back from the girl's forehead.

'Won't be long now, my bird,' Annie said.

During the next half-hour the contractions grew stronger and more frequent. Farah clutched Jess's hand as they both blew quick breaths through pursed lips.

Then suddenly Farah curled forward, her head lifting off the cushion as she strained.

Jess swivelled round, slid her arm under Farah's shoulders to support her, and saw Farah's lips draw back from her teeth as a guttural sound emerged from her throat.

'Hold on, bird, just a minute,' Annie's gloved hands were busy between Farah's raised knees. 'All right, push now. That's right, my sweetheart. And one more.'

Farah hunched and groaned, trembling with effort.

Jess saw a smile spread over Annie's face. 'There we are. You've got a handsome baby boy.'

Wonder smoothed all the pain from Farah's face as Annie gave the baby a little shake. The tiny mouth opened and a bleat of protest emerged.

'Got a fine pair of lungs on him,' Annie said, laying the small pink slippery body on Farah's deflated stomach.

'Oh! Isn't he beautiful?' Farah breathed.

Her eyes stinging, Jess nodded, flexing the hand Farah had crushed. 'He's perfect.'

From downstairs the sound of 'While Shepherds Watched Their Flocks By Night' thundered through the closed doors. Jess thought of Morwenna singing her heart out and blinked away tears.

She, Tom, and Morwenna had been in the same

188

class at the village school. But as far as Jess knew Morwenna had never had a boyfriend and was now unlikely ever to have a child. Her life revolved around her job at a builder's merchants in the town two miles away, the choir, and looking after her endlessly complaining mother.

Looking at Farah's glowing face as she gently stroked her son's damp swirl of black hair with a careful finger, Jess thought of her own sons. Sam in Australia teaching at a sports academy, spending every spare moment surfing, and Rob, married with a baby girl and currently on rotation in A&E at the city hospital.

'Jess,' Farah's soft voice broke into her thoughts. 'Will you tell Khalid? He's been so worried.'

Annie glanced up. 'He can come in and see for hisself soon as I've made you comfortable and tidied things away. Jess, this young lady could do with something to eat and a cup of tea. I wouldn't mind one myself.'

As Jess opened the door, Khalid and Tom both jumped to their feet.

'Khalid, you have a fine baby boy.'

'A son?' Khalid's voice cracked. 'Farah?'

'She's fine. Tired but very happy and waiting to see you. Annie is just making her comfortable.' She glanced down the stairs and saw Gill and Viv peering up.

'Everything all right?' Gill asked.

Khalid leaned forward, his tired face alight with pride and relief. 'We have a son.'

'That's wonderful. Congratulations,' Gill said. 'Your girl all right, is she?'

He nodded. 'Jess says they are both fine. I will see them soon.'

'Proper job, my 'andsome,' Viv beamed.

'Come on,' Gill nudged her. "Oh Come All Ye Faithful" was the last carol. Be like feeding time at the zoo in a minute.' She switched off the bubbling urn, rinsed two huge brown teapots, added teabags, then filled them with boiling water. Viv carried the last loaded plate to the hatch worktop.

Khalid seized Jess's hand between both of his. 'Thank you so much.' Then turning he grabbed Tom's hand and shook it hard. 'Without your kindness ... We can never –'

'Baby got here safe and mother's fine,' Tom grinned. 'That's enough for me.'

'Me too,' Jess nodded. 'I'm sorry you had to run away. But I'm glad you ended up here. I wouldn't have missed this for anything. Would you like another cup of tea? I'm going to get one for Annie and some supper for Farah.'

He shook his head. 'Will Annie be long, do you think?' As he spoke the door opened and Annie beamed at him.

'In you come. You give your girl a kiss then you can watch me bath your son.'

As the door closed behind him, Jess walked down the stairs with Tom close behind. At the bottom he put his arm around her shoulders.

'Been some night, hasn't it? And not over yet.'

Applause erupted, loud and prolonged, on the other side of the hatch.

'Viv,' Jess leapt forward. 'Don't open the hatch for a minute. I've got to take –'

'Don't fret, bird,' Gill called. 'Tray's ready. Two cups of tea and two plates filled with a bit of everything.' She thrust it into Jess's hands. 'Up you go.'

Viv waited for Jess to come down and as soon as she stepped off the bottom stair, unbolted the hatch and folded the doors back. Noise burst into the kitchen like a breaking wave.

While Viv and Gill poured tea and pushed cups and saucers through the hatch, Tom replaced empty plates with others piled high with sandwiches, sausage rolls, portions of quiche, scones topped with jam and cream, and slices of various cakes.

Filling the sink with hot soapy water, Jess started to wash up, her euphoria giving way to concern.

'Hey, don't look so worried.' Tom bumped her shoulder with his. 'Where's the tea towels?'

'Second drawer down,' she nodded, her hands deep in the frothy water. 'Tom, they can't stay here.'

'They'll have to until everyone's gone home and the pub's shut for the night.' Drying the cups and saucers he put them on the cleared worktop ready for Gill, keeping his back to the open hatch so no one but Jess could hear him. 'Can I phone from your place? The friends they were meeting in France ought to be told what's happened. And I need to make another call.'

191

Jess turned her head, looked into his eyes. 'You're not thinking of taking them across on *Marie-Louise?*'

He grinned. 'You always were sharp as a tack.' The grin faded. 'I'll be straight with you. I did think about it –'

'Tom, you can't.'

'Let me finish, woman,' he said mildly. 'I said I thought about it. But it's too risky. They've got passports but the baby hasn't. If we arrived at Roscoff or Cherbourg and they haven't got paperwork proving the baby is theirs, the border police and God knows who else would be called in and they could be charged with kidnap or child trafficking.'

His words hit Jess like a punch, stopping her breath. 'No!'

'If that happened it would wreck any hope of keeping their whereabouts secret. It also crossed my mind to sail over to some quiet cove on the Brittany coast and put them ashore. But if they were picked up it would mean police, courts, all kinds of trouble. They'd likely be put on the first ferry or flight back to the UK.'

Jess was awed. 'You certainly have thought about it.'

'I'm not just a pretty face.'

'Jess!' Jess looked round and saw Gill nod towards Morwenna who had slipped into the kitchen through the back door that Viv immediately relocked. She was carrying a man's unturned cap in front of her. Her face was flushed deep rose and her eyes were shining. Recognising the cap as Dennis's, Jess saw it was full

192

of money.

'What's this?'

'I took up a collection. I said it was for the homeless. Well it is.'

Cupping her face, Tom kissed her soundly. 'You are a jewel.' She blushed crimson.

Jess wiped her hands on Tom's tea towel. 'Mor, come with me.'

'Hang on a minute.' He poured the money into a plastic tub and handed it to Morwenna. 'Dennis will want his cap.'

Jess pushed Morwenna towards the stairs. 'Don't be long,' she murmured to Tom. 'I want to know what you're planning.'

On the landing she knocked then opened the door. 'May we come in?' Annie had pushed the makeshift curtain back towards the window removing the barrier.

Khalid rose from his chair facing Farah. 'The lady singer,' he smiled. 'Come and meet our son.'

A lump swelled in Jess's throat at the expression on Morwenna's face as she looked down at the baby in Farah's arms.

'Oh, the dear of him! Isn't he just handsome?' She thrust the tub into Khalid's hands but spoke to Farah. ''Tisn't much but it all helps, don't it?'

Jess saw shock blank Khalid's face as he looked from the money to Morwenna.

'What is it?' Farah asked. Khalid showed her. 'Oh!' Tears spilled down Farah's cheeks but her smile was radiant. 'When he's older I will tell him about the night he was born. You've all been so kind.' She lifted the baby to kiss him, her shoulders shaking. Putting the tub down, Khalid crouched beside her, his head close to hers as he stroked her hair.

'Come on, Mor,' Jess drew her towards the door. 'You must be parched. Gill's got a cup of tea waiting for you downstairs. We heard your solos.'

'You did?' Morwenna glanced back at couple and baby one final time. Then Jess closed the door and they started down to the kitchen.

'Oh damn,' Jess muttered seeing Bessie Richards at the hatch, her eyes bright with curiosity as she heaped a plate with different types of cake.

'What you doing up there?'

'Trying to make space for Margaret's screens,' Jess improvised before Morwenna could speak. 'There isn't room behind the stage.'

'How's that then?'

'Harry's storing the card tables back there. He wants them easier to reach.'

'Well, make sure you get him to carry them up. You shouldn't have to do it.' She waddled away with her full plate and Jess released the breath she'd been holding.

Reaching the bottom, Morwenna hurried over to Gill. 'Isn't he just gorgeous? Dear little soul. I've never seen a newborn. He's so tiny. Those little hands and that lovely black hair.'

'My Mark was born with a lovely thatch of hair like that. He kept it too.' Gill pulled out a stool and patted it. 'Take the weight off, Mor. Tea's fresh.' She moved the steaming cup forward then put a plate of food beside it. 'You did some wonderful job tonight. We could hear you. Sounded beautiful you did.'

As Viv chatted to people returning empty cups and plates to the hatch, Jess joined Tom at the sink.

'What did she think of the baby?' he asked as she picked up the tea towel.

'The look on her face –' Jess looked away shaking her head as she swallowed hard.

'Been one hell of an evening hasn't it, girl?'

Taking a deep breath Jess wiped her eyes. 'So, if you can't take them across by boat –'

'I could, but not without papers for the baby. Besides, sailing over in *Marie-Louise* could take up to twenty-four hours depending on winds and where we landed. Better to fly them across.'

Jess clutched a half-wiped plate to her chest. 'Fly?'

'Did you ever meet Roger Tregenna?'

'I don't think so.'

'His father used to over-winter his boat at the yard. I've known him years. He's a flying instructor up at Bodmin Airfield.'

'I've seen those little planes flying from Land's End airport. But they're only two-seaters.'

'Not Roger's. He does charter work as well. He's got a four-seater Cessna Skyhawk.'

'Even assuming he agrees –'

'I'll persuade him. He owes me a favour.'

'Yes but how much will it cost? We can't expect him to do it for free.'

Tom lifted one shoulder. 'I won't know till I ask.'

'Go and phone him. The front door key is in my

right-hand pocket. While you're there you'd better phone Khalid's friends and tell them what's happened.'

Wiping his hands on the tea towel, he shrugged into his jacket, held up the key, then took the stairs two at a time. Moments later he hurried down, pushing a piece of paper into his pocket.

'Oi, where're you skiving off to?' Gill demanded as she picked up a stack of dirty dishes and started towards the sink. Jess saw him pause, speaking softly. Gill nodded towards the kitchen door. 'Oh, right. Go on then.'

Morwenna carried her plate and cup to Jess. 'Want me to dry them do you?'

'No, it's all right, Mor. Most of it's done. You'd better get on home. You did a brilliant job tonight.'

'I'd sooner stay.' There was yearning on her face. Then she sighed and went to fetch her coat. 'But Mother will fret if I'm late.' She glanced towards the stairs. 'Where will they go, Jess?'

'Tom's gone to make some phone calls. He's got a plan to help them reach their friends.'

Excitement flickered across Morwenna's tired face. 'Will you tell me what happens?'

'Of course I will. I'll phone you at work and you can call in at my place on your way home.'

Morwenna buttoned her coat. 'I'll never forget tonight, not till my dying day.'

''Night, Mor,' Jess, Gill and Viv called.

As the back door closed behind Morwenna, Gill leaned over the worktop and peered out through the

196

hatch. 'The choir's gone. There's just a few stragglers chatting near the door. I'll go and get the rest of the dishes.' Picking up an empty tray she unlocked the door into the hall and left it open.

'Jess, I've put the leftovers in those two plastic containers,' Viv said then began wiping down the worktops.

'Any sign of Harry?' Jess asked as Gill returned and unloaded the tray.

'You got to be kidding. He'll be over in the pub until Alan calls time.'

Jess sighed. 'Looks like we'll be folding the card tables and stacking the chairs.'

They had almost finished when Tom arrived back. He came through the front door and locked it behind him.

'I called in at the pub and got the keys off Harry. I told him we still had a bit to do so I'd lock up to save him hanging around.'

'He didn't mind?' Jess was surprised.

Tom grinned. 'Mind? He's propped up against the bar with Brian Rowse putting the world to rights. Alan will need a crowbar to shift them. Come on in the kitchen.'

'And me?' Gill asked.

''Course, Viv too. We'd never have got through tonight without the pair of you.'

Even with the hatch and both kitchen doors closed Tom kept his voice low. 'I rang Khalid's friend, Masoud. To begin with he wouldn't even admit to knowing Khalid and Farah. But when I told him about the baby, and that we were doing our best to get them across to France within the next twenty-four hours he apologised. He works for an IT company and can get Khalid work. His wife, Nasrin, is a doctor. She'll make sure Farah and the baby get proper care.

'I have to phone them again as soon as we know where Khalid and Farah will be touching down.'

'You've spoken to Roger?' Jess asked.

Tom nodded. 'He's free in the morning. Though he's booked to give a flying lesson at two he'll postpone it if necessary.'

'That's very good of him. Obviously he'll have to be paid.'

'He said as long as we cover the fuel and landing charges, he's happy.'

Gill's brows climbed. 'Dear life, you surely got a good friend there.'

Tom grinned. 'He loves to fly and this will be a welcome break in routine. His words, not mine.' He caught Jess's eye and she grinned.

'Where will you take them?'

'Nowhere until the baby's birth has been registered. Everything has to be legal.'

'The register office in town is open Thursdays from 9.30 until 11,' Viv said. 'I was in there after Father died back in March.'

'I'll have Khalid on the doorstep at 9.25 with his passport. Annie wrote down the date and time the baby was born, his weight, and his parents' names. She put the village as his place of birth.'

'Bless her for thinking of that,' Jess said.

'As soon as we get back, we'll pick up Farah and the baby and drive to Bodmin airfield.'

'Yes, but where are they flying *to*?'

'Roger said if he flies them into a quiet airfield like Quimper there'll be fewer people around but they may be remembered. Cherbourg is much busier but they'll be just two more in the crowd. The flight will take around forty-five minutes depending on the wind.' He pushed away from the worktop he'd been leaning against. 'It's their lives, their choice. I'll go and ask.'

Gill laid her hand on Jess's forearm. 'Look, if there's nothing else Viv and me can do we'll get on home. I aren't used to all this excitement.'

Jess hugged her. 'Thanks so much.'

'Mind you let us know what happens.'

'I will, I promise. Night, Viv. And thanks.'

'Wouldn't have missed it for the world. This is what Christmas is really about, isn't it?'

After they'd gone, Tom turned the key and followed Jess upstairs. 'What are we going to do with them tonight? They can't stay here in the dark. And if they leave the light on someone will notice.'

'I'll have them,' Jess said.

'Jess, your cottage is right in the middle of the village. You've got Ivy next door. There's no way we'll get them out in the morning without someone seeing. They'll be safer at mine. My nearest neighbour is a hundred yards away. Chris will be over for the weekend. But he's not coming until Friday evening.'

An hour later, while Farah was in the bathroom, Jess and Tom made up his bed with fresh sheets. After a single glance exchanged as she shook out the bottom sheet, Jess kept her head bent as they smoothed and tucked. She wondered if his silence meant that he too found the intimacy unsettling.

'I didn't expect to be doing this tonight,' he said. 'Not for strangers anyway. I mean, I hoped one day we – but there's no rush. Not that you would have had to – I'd have done all this before –'

'Tom,' Jess smothered a grin. 'You're in deep enough. Stop digging.'

'Right. I was just saying. You know, to keep in mind for the future –'

'Tom!' While she put a fresh cover on the duvet, he emptied one of the dresser drawers, padding it with a soft blanket as a makeshift cot.

By the time Khalid emerged from the bathroom, Farah was propped up in bed nursing the baby. Jess placed two mugs of cocoa and a bottle of water on the bedside table.

'Goodnight. If you need anything we're just downstairs.'

'Thank you –' Khalid began.

'It was our pleasure,' she cut him short with a smile. 'Try to sleep. You'll have another long day tomorrow.' Closing the door she went down to the sitting room.

Tom was kneeling in front of the woodburner feeding in more logs. Seeing the long deep sofa took Jess back to her teens when this had been his parents' house. Then the floral pattern on the loose covers had been crisp and bright. Now, faded by sunlight and washing, the colours were blurred pastel shades. Soft cushions in a flattened heap at one end showed his favourite place to watch TV.

Sinking onto the sofa she released a heartfelt sigh. Dusting off his hands on the seat of his jeans Tom sat down and gave her a gentle push so she fell sideways onto the cushions.

'Stay.' He lifted her legs, eased off her shoes and started massaging her feet.

She turned so her head and shoulders rested comfortably on the cushions 'Oh, that's wonderful.'

'Some carol concert that was.'

Jess nodded. 'I'm shattered.' As his strong fingers kneaded, she closed her eyes and felt herself drift. There was something she had intended to ask him. But as the stress of the evening melted away she couldn't remember what it was.

She woke with a start and in the dim light of a table lamp on the bookcase saw Tom sprawled sound asleep in the armchair by the woodburner.

She sat up and the blanket he had laid over her fell to the floor. The soft sound woke him. For a long moment they looked at one another. Then Jess glanced at her watch and winced.

'Where did the night go?' She swung her feet to the floor.

Tom stood up. 'You know where the clean towels are. I'll put the kettle on and fetch Annie.'

While Khalid showered and shaved, Annie bathed the baby, then Farah showered and dressed. Tom prepared breakfast. Jess stripped the bed and loaded the washing machine.

At ten past nine Tom and Khalid left for town, dropping Annie off on the way. Farah fed the baby and Jess washed up. At five minutes to ten she heard the throaty rumble of Tom's pick-up and at ten fifteen they were on their way to Bodmin Airfield.

An overnight shower had left the air crisp and clear. A gentle breeze pushed cotton wool clouds across a sky the colour of forget-me-nots.

The pick-up had a crew cab that seated four. Jess rode in front next to Tom, with Khalid, Farah, and the baby in the rear where they were less likely to be seen.

The roads were quiet. The rush to school and work was over and Christmas shoppers were still at home.

In the back Khalid and Farah talked softly, their voices blending with the engine noise. Jess remembered and turned to Tom.

'Is now a good time to tell me?' As he glanced at her she prompted. 'Chris? Yesterday? In court?'

After a moment's hesitation he gave a brief nod. 'Mick Carter gave evidence for the coastguard. Mick's a good bloke. I've known him years. He told the magistrates he believed the tip-off had come from one of the smugglers.'

'Why would they do that?'

'Mick said in his opinion Chris was a throwaway. It was worth it to the gang to shop him and lose a few thousand cigarettes. That would keep the coastguard busy while the rest of the cargo was put ashore somewhere else. Mick told me if it had been up to him he'd have given Chris a good talking to and let him off. But now with these new tougher laws to tackle tobacco and cigarette smuggling, he didn't have a choice. He had to prosecute.'

'And Chris pleaded guilty?'

Tom nodded. 'Not that he could have done anything else seeing he was caught with the stuff. But his guilty plea pleased the magistrates. The chairlady, or whatever they're called now, said it showed he was taking responsibility for what he'd done and as it's his first offence they gave him a six-month referral order.'

'How is he?' Jess saw how talking about it had deepened lines of strain across his forehead and the outer corners of his eyes.

'Shaken, and so he damn well should be. Whoever got him into it gave him twenty quid with a promise of eighty more once the load was safely ashore. They knew they weren't going to give him another penny. They knew he wouldn't "grass" either.'

'How could they be sure?' Jess asked, then realised. 'They threatened him.'

'That's what I thought. The magistrates asked who got him into it. But he refused to say. The lady in charge asked if he'd been threatened with violence. But it wasn't him they were going to hurt. The bastards said they would burn the yard.'

'Oh Tom,' Jess murmured, appalled.

'Poor little sod. He thought it would be easy money and he's saving up to buy a car soon as he's passed his test.' He rubbed his forehead, sighed. 'Susan says it's my fault. If I'd been a better father, spent more time with him –'

'Hang on a minute. When your father died the boatyard was in desperate straits financially.'

'That's true, but –'

'You were working eighteen-hour days to keep it going. Then Susan wanted a divorce –'

'Because I was always working.'

'To save the business that paid for the house she's living in. Tom, you did the best you could in the circumstances. Stop beating yourself up.'

The smile warmed his eyes as he glanced at her. 'You always say the right thing.'

She shrugged. 'It's the truth. What is this referral order?'

'Chris has to go in front of a panel and sign up to a contract of work in the community. Jobs like helping the village volunteer group clean out choked ditches and trim overgrown footpaths. The person supervising him will report back to the panel. I told the magistrates I'll give him weekend work at the yard.' Tom snorted. 'I offered him a job when he turned sixteen but he didn't want to know.'

'Let me guess, he wanted to hang out with his mates. What did he say this time?'

'Jumped at it. I think knowing they deliberately set him up, then having to go to court, has given him one hell of a shock. He also let on that he doesn't like Susan's new man bossing him around. So it looks like he'll be spending more time with me.'

'That will be good for both of you.'

'I told him straight he won't get special treatment. But if he does the crap jobs without complaining and

204

shows interest I'll take him on as an apprentice.'

'What did he say?'

'Not a lot. You know what teenagers are.'

She laughed. 'I remember it well.'

'If I ever get hold of the bastards who set him up … Just as well I won't, else it would be me in court. Chris knows he's been lucky. Still, if he buys a car with money he's earned, he won't want to wreck it.' He looked across at her with a wry grin. 'When do you stop worrying?'

Jess laughed. 'You don't. It arrives when they are born and it's always there at the back of your mind.'

'Thanks for that.'

'You did ask.' Jess patted his forearm. 'I'm glad for you, Tom.'

'Here we are.'

Roger met them at the door to the tiny terminal building. Wearing an olive-green flying suit he was lean and wiry with a narrow face, blue eyes, and a grey crew cut.

'You made good time.'

Introductions were made, hands shaken, and he smiled at the sleeping baby. After he had examined their passports and the baby's pristine birth certificate he returned them to Khalid.

'The forecast is excellent so it should be a quick, comfortable flight. I've already done all the checks so we're good to go.'

While Khalid pumped Tom's hand, his voice rough and incoherent, Jess hugged Farah whose face was wet with tears.

'Thank you, Jess. We will never forget, never. '

'Be happy.' Jess bent and gently kissed the baby's forehead. His skin was warm and soft and his sweet baby smell brought back vivid memories of Rob and Sam just a few hours old and herself exhausted and euphoric. She stepped back, her vision blurred, and felt Tom's arm encircle her shoulder and draw her close.

She wiped her eyes and a few moments later they watched the red and white plane speed down the runway and climb into the sky.

Back in the pick-up Tom started the engine then turned to her. 'Doing anything special on Christmas Day?'

She shook her head. 'Sam will be in Oz. Rob and Fiona are having their first Christmas with Helen in their own home which I think is a wise decision. I'll phone Rob and Fiona this evening and ask if I can have Helen for a day sometime between now and next Wednesday.' She pulled a face. 'When Rob rang yesterday I turned him down.'

'You've got jobs to finish.'

'Yes, I have. But after last night –'

When she broke off he nodded and she knew he understood.

'I can work while she has her nap, and I'll put in a couple of evenings. What about you? Are you doing anything special?'

He shook his head. 'Chris will be over this weekend. But Susan wants him with her on Christmas Day.'

Jess nodded.

'So I thought –' He cleared his throat. 'I was wondering – how about you and me doing nothing special at my place?'

She met his gaze and felt her heart give a little leap. Maybe it wasn't too soon after all.

For more information about other
Accent Press titles

please visit

www.accentpress.co.uk

Printed in Great
Britain
by Amazon